MORE THAN A PORTRAIT

When Jane is offered a job in northern Italy, with its promise of sunshine and colour, mountains and romantic scenery, her adventurous spirit can hardly refuse. Then she meets her employer: the unpredictable, pompous and dictatorial Duncan Frobisher. Sparks immediately fly between them, and Jane comes to know more than her fair share of elation and black depression before her temporary employment comes to an end . . .

ADE

Please renew or return items by the date
shown on your receipt

www.hertsdirect.org/libraries

Renewals and enquiries: 0300 123 4049
Textphone for hearing or 0300 123 4041
speech impaired users:

L32

46 418 374 5

DIANA DENNISON

MORE THAN A PORTRAIT

Complete and Unabridged

LINFORD
Leicester

First published in Great Britain in 1975 by
Robert Hale & Company
London

First Linford Edition
published 2014
by arrangement with
Robert Hale & Company
London

A catalogue record for this book is available
from the British Library.

ISBN 978–1–4448–1899–4

Published by
F. A. Thorpe (Publishing)
Anstey, Leicestershire

Set by Words & Graphics Ltd.
Anstey, Leicestershire
Printed and bound in Great Britain by
T. J. International Ltd., Padstow, Cornwall

This book is printed on acid-free paper

1

The bus stopped conveniently adjacent to a puddle, which didn't exactly help Jane to overcome her disgruntlement with the fine drizzle that seemed to wet everything so much more efficiently than pelting rain ever managed to do. Just as she turned in at the drive leading to the Greshams' house a car turned through the same gateway and she had to jump aside quickly to avoid being hit by it.

The car skidded to a halt on the wet gravel; and a tall man jumped out and ran back to her.

'I'm terribly sorry if I frightened you. Are you all right?' The pleasant voice was full of lively concern.

Jane's mounting irritation with the weather had been dispelled by the sudden fright so that instead of the retort that was rising to her lips the culprit received a reassuring smile.

'Oh, yes,' she assured him. 'It was my own fault. I shouldn't have been walking in the middle of the drive, but these trees do drip so.'

'Well, thanks for taking it that way.' The relief in his voice was obvious. 'As we seem to be bound for the same place, at least let me save you from the trees and make amends by giving you a lift to the door.' So saying he propelled her firmly to the stationary car without waiting for a reply. Jane felt that her murmured thanks were somewhat superfluous.

'By the way, I'd better introduce myself. I'm Max, Max Frobisher — Celia Gresham's brother,' he added when he sensed rather than saw that Jane was none the wiser for his first statement.

'And I'm Jane Marten,' she told him guardedly, scanning his face for a reaction to this intelligence. A not at all unpleasant face, she was forced to admit grudgingly.

Whatever reaction she had expected, it was not the obviously spontaneous exclamation of pleased surprise that accompanied his sudden smile.

'What a coincidence,' he laughed, 'that you should be the very person I have come here to meet. I hope you won't hold the manner of our meeting against me in future.'

This certainly was not the attitude of a man dragged into a party to escort an unknown female having the doubtful recommendation that she was a highly specialised schoolteacher. Jane was frankly puzzled, but there was no time for questions or explanations before the door of the house opened to welcome them as the car came to a standstill.

The Greshams were not close friends, but Jane had come to know them increasingly well through her work. Little Tony Gresham was born deaf, and therefore dumb. Jane had first met his parents when they decided to send Tony to the special school where she taught children with speech defects to overcome their disabilities and to join the world of talkers. Her instant affection for the child had led to a warm friendship with his parents, who were almost overwhelmingly grateful for her part in teaching their little son to speak.

After Celia Gresham introduced her to the group of guests already collected in the spacious drawing-room, Jane found herself seated apart from the others for a moment. She enjoyed watching other people and idly wondering about their occupations and various relationships to each other. But she was not to be left alone for long she saw: Max Frobisher was crossing the room towards her. Watching him speaking to several guests as he moved closer, she became aware of his undeniable charm and a definite air of confidence in his manner. She also noticed that he was unquestionably the most handsome man in the room.

'At least I've been presented with an acceptable partner,' she told herself with a wry smile, as she watched his steady progress in her direction.

Celia Gresham and her brother

arrived at Jane's side simultaneously. Under the influence of the other woman's smile Jane found the last vestige of her earlier irritation fading away until she, too, was smiling warmly.

'Miss Marten, please talk to Max and tell him about your work. I know that I'm asking you to talk *shop* off duty, but these doctors never seem to be any use at small talk. All a poor hostess can do is to avoid them like the plague or admit defeat and find them someone to talk their own particular *shop* with.' Celia Gresham looked up at her tall brother with a teasing smile. 'The situation becomes more difficult when the offender happens to be one's own brother. Don't you agree, Max?'

Max's answering laugh was gay and affectionate. 'I'm sorry for you, my poor sister,' he teased. 'You know perfectly well that I'm quite capable of being off duty, as you put it. Now if I were Duncan you really would have Max's sympathy with your problem.'

As the brother and sister laughed

together at their shared joke, Jane looked at Max with a new interest. She was mildly surprised to learn that he was a member of the profession with which she came in frequent contact in the course of her daily work. His light-hearted confidence would be the greatest tonic that he could offer to any of his patients, she felt.

Celia Gresham turned to include Jane in their laughter. 'Duncan is my other brother,' she explained.

'The strong and silent type who takes life rather more seriously than I do,' added Max. They all three laughed this time.

'Anyway, Miss Marten, Max really is very interested in what you've done for Tony. Please tell him about your methods. He'll be a much better informed audience than I am when you try to explain to me.'

'I expect Miss Marten would like to forget her work for a while.' Max was smiling at her as he spoke.

Jane glanced up at the two who were

so alike as they stood beside her.

'I've had a long rest from my work recently, and it's not the sort of work one forgets easily,' she replied to the implied question.

Celia Gresham turned to Jane again.

'Well, at least I know that you two are more capable of interesting each other than some of my other guests are, so I'll leave you while I do my duty elsewhere.'

When his sister left them, Max turned to Jane with a guilty smile playing about the corners of his mouth.

'If you really don't mind talking about it now I honestly am interested in how your sort of school tackles the problem of children like Tony.' He bent forward as he continued to speak. 'Two years ago he was just an inarticulate bundle of child, but when I came home last week I found a happy imp of mischief, quite ready to hold a conversation, mostly about yourself,' he added with a grin.

'After six months' absence?' she

challenged his flattery. 'But you're quite right about the talking. He can communicate very well when he wants to make himself understood.'

'Don't I just know what you mean by that!' Max exclaimed. 'I work a lot with handicapped children, too, and I know just how infuriating the little devils can be. Sometimes you know full well that they are capable of doing twice as much, if only they could be persuaded to give their full attention for two consecutive minutes. It certainly taxes one's patience at times.'

His intention to draw Jane into conversation was amply rewarded. She had listened to him with parted lips and was quite ready to offer her own contribution.

'I've thought a lot about this business of trying to make them concentrate,' she said, 'and I've come to the conclusion that their inability to do so is their most important safety valve against our trying to push them forward too fast.'

8

The two of them were off to a good start on a subject that they both found intensely interesting. It wasn't until someone interrupted to announce dinner that they realised how engrossed they had become in their own shared world.

Jane had visited the Greshams' home before, but this was the first formal invitation she had received to their gracious house in an expensive district of her own home town. The 'little meal' that Celia had invited her to share turned out to be a full-scale dinner for eight couples. Jane found herself rapidly forgetting her own problems as she enjoyed the pleasure of the company and the perfectly served meal at the long, highly polished table. As Tony's schoolteacher she had often visited the house before, but she had only seen Celia Gresham's small sitting-room. The spacious rooms that she saw now were a revelation to her. She had realised that the Greshams were rich by modern standards, but this almost outdated standard of living was something for which she was not prepared.

As she talked with her dinner neighbours, both unknown to her, Jane felt more alive and interested in the people about her than she had done at any time in the past six months. Her conversation with Max Frobisher had shown her very clearly just how much she had missed the stimulation of her work. It was not that she resented the interruption of her work that her sister's illness had caused, but she was finding it very difficult to pick up the threads of her former life.

When Eileen had been told that it would be necessary for her to spend at least six months in bed it had been inevitable that Jane should give up her own hard-earned teaching post to become her sister's housekeeper. The girls' mother was eager to help her married daughter, and indignant that Jane's career should be interrupted by the domestic crisis, but gentle persuasion had shown her that her own failing health would be no match for the robust health of Eileen's two lively toddlers.

After dinner there was coffee, served in the drawing-room. Before conversation got underway after the move from the dining table, Max Frobisher was beside Jane again and guiding her to a pair of isolated chairs in the bay of the window.

As soon as they were seated he spoke without preamble.

'Now, Jane, I may call you that, please?' He took the permission for granted and continued without waiting for a reply. 'I want to talk to you about your work and find out whether you have any definite plans for the future.'

Janet met this devastatingly direct approach with an amused though puzzled smile.

'My work?' she queried uncertainly. 'I really haven't had time to make any plans; there aren't many jobs going in the middle of the school year.'

He nodded and smiled briefly. 'Good. That's all I wanted to know.

Now I'll reveal the dastardly plot. I came to England specially to meet you, you know.'

Jane, who certainly did not know, was thoroughly startled by this announcement, but he gave her no time to question his words.

'My brother is an orthopaedic surgeon. He runs a small clinic for disabled children and just now he has six children who are deaf in addition to their other troubles. I have come back with orders to find a specialist teacher for them.' There was at last a pause while Jane waited for him to continue, knowing full well what he was about to say.

'Will you take the job, Jane?'

So this was why she had been asked to meet Max Frobisher. She had to say something while her mind was occupied with a rapid review of what he had just said. From among the varied tantalising impressions left by his words she caught at one point which she had not understood.

'You said that you have 'come back' to find someone for this post. What did you mean by that?'

He looked completely surprised.

'Oh, didn't you know? I took it for granted that you would know about us from Celia. The clinic is in Italy — the northern lake district to be specific.' His voice took on a highly artificial tone. 'It is situated high on the mountains above a particularly attractive lake — a truly splendid location.' In his normal and very pleasing voice he added, 'You'd love the place I'm sure.'

A rising tide of excitement gripped at the romantic side of Jane's rather practical nature. To continue the work that she loved with this dynamic man for whom she was rapidly developing a strong liking was excitement enough, but to add to this the chance to live in Italy with its promise of sunshine and colour, mountains and romantic scenery, was to offer a prospect which any imaginative girl would find hard to resist.

'This is such a surprise, Max,' she protested laughingly. 'You must know that I can't answer right away, just like that.' Somehow the use of his name came easily and naturally, a fact which mildly surprised the usually reserved Jane.

2

'Why not? Surely it's a simple yes or no.' He obviously found nothing unusual about the informal style of address.

'How easy people always make these things sound!' she exclaimed. 'It may be simple once you have it all weighed out, but I haven't had a chance to think about it at all yet.'

'Surely there's nothing to think about. You've already left the school, haven't you? If it's money you're worried about, you needn't — Duncan's quite solvent.'

Jane laughed outright at this. 'Oh, you're quite impossible,' she told him. 'I'll let you know by the end of the week and that's my final word.' As he was about to speak another thought made her interrupt him. 'But what about your brother? Surely he will want to know something about me before you make such a decision.'

'That's all settled. Celia gave you such a glowing testimonial that I have *carte blanche* from Duncan to engage you on any reasonable terms, if I think fit. So it really is very easy, you see.'

In spite of herself Jane could not help laughing at this admission of preformed plans.

'Did it ever occur to you or your brother that I might not wish to go out into darkest Italy?' Although her face and voice were perfectly grave there was mischief dancing in her eyes as she met his surprised stare.

'But you will come, won't you?'

Jane refused to be led into an unconsidered answer. The many questions that had arisen in her mind were not to be answered before the guests began to leave. Max had to be content with her promise to contact him during the coming week. She was grateful when he insisted on driving her home, but she was still adamant in her refusal to give him a definite answer that evening.

16

For all her protests to Max that she needed time to think about the idea, Jane knew quite well that if the details of the post were reasonable she would be willing to go to Italy.

⋆ ⋆ ⋆

So it was that with a sense of adventure, and few misgivings, Jane found herself airborne on the flight to Milan and a new life; in a community where she had not a single friend or even an acquaintance. At last she had time to relax and for the first time in three hectic weeks of hurried preparation; weeks of shopping, packing and continuous correspondence with Max Frobisher and his brother in Italy. It had come to a climax in a gay evening with Max himself when they had wined and dined together at his insistent request; to give her a memorable farewell, he said.

The letters from Duncan Frobisher had been business-like to the point of terseness and quite unrevealing. As the plane purred gently through the sky Jane had time to wonder about the man whom she expected to meet her in Milan. She had been told that the patients of the clinic were children of various ages who suffered from physical disabilities caused either by injuries or, in some cases, by pre-natal malformations. Some surgery was carried out at the Villa Alto clinic, she knew from the letters, but in most cases the children were transferred from hospitals when it became apparent that they required extended specialist care. How an English surgeon — an orthopaedic specialist, Max had said — came to be in charge of a remote Italian clinic was not explained. Jane knew all the necessary details of her new post, but nothing about the man with whom she was to work, except that he was Max Frobisher's brother.

Jane's lips parted in an unconscious smile as she thought of Max. The young man seated next to her glanced up at that moment and allowed his gaze to rest appreciatively on the face of his fellow passenger. Jane was watching with fascination the formation of the clouds below and she was far too well occupied to notice the interested scrutiny of her neighbour. This was her first experience of flying, so she was far too excited to realise that the wind at the airport had lifted her usually smooth dark curls about her face, and excitement had brought an unaccustomed colour to her cheeks.

More than one person spared an admiring glance for Jane's animated face, but she was oblivious of her fellow passengers as she sat in speculative thought and gazed at the cloud which seemed so solid and yet was as intangible as a dream.

The stewardess was bending over her asking if she would like a cocktail before lunch was served. Bringing her thoughts back from their flight into the future, Jane recalled Max's amused tolerance at her lack of appreciation for alcohol. If she was to live in Italy, he had assured her, she must learn to like the national drinks. Laughing inwardly at herself, she ordered a Cinzano Bianco and settled down to enjoy its light freshness.

A slight movement at her side made her glance for the first time at her travelling companion. It was with a sense of surprise that she noticed that despite his very English clothes the young man was unmistakably Italian.

Their lunch arrived at that moment and as he handed her tray across to her the young man spoke for the first time.

'Excuse me, may I ask if you are Miss Jane Marten?'

'Why, yes.' Jane's surprise must have been eloquently expressed on her face. Her companion laughed at her astonished expression and hastened to explain.

'I am sorry to surprise you so, but I was told that you would be travelling on this flight. Dr Frobisher wrote asking me to look out for you and to escort you from Milan.'

'Oh, I see. So you know Dr Frobisher in Italy.'

'That is so,' he agreed, with a pleasing little bow which was somewhat curtailed by the presence of the tray across his lap. 'Allow me to introduce myself. I am Mario Ronelli. I too am a doctor and work with Dr Frobisher at the Villa Alto clinic.'

Jane was delighted with this news. Here at last was her first real contact with the new work which she had undertaken so precipitately. With an effort she curbed her womanly curiosity which prompted at least ten immediate questions.

'You must tell me about the clinic,' she said eagerly. 'I scarcely know anything about it.'

'The clinic you will see soon enough,' was the reply. 'Please tell me how you, an English girl, have come to join us.'

The smile that he flashed at her held the promise of all her most romantic dreams of Italy. She found his eager curiosity about herself only flattering and not at all embarrassing. The unaccustomed interest and the gallantry with which her companion saw that she had every comfort was stimulating. As they flew through the clouds above France, Jane told Mario Ronelli enough of the past weeks to make an interesting story. To tell a stranger so much about herself was something that she had never done before, but the intimate atmosphere of the aircraft cabin was conducive to quick-flowering friendship.

She had very little time to think about anything but getting through the customs formalities at Milan before Mario had hurried her into a waiting car. As they moved swiftly through the traffic they passed an imposing archway that, to Jane, looked like a grand but quite near relation to London's Marble Arch, which she had passed only a few hours ago. According to Mario, this one was known as the Arch of Peace.

As they crossed the Lombardy Plain

and made for the foothills of the Alps, Mario pointed out various landmarks and explained how the many mulberry trees that they saw were the mainstay of the silk industry at Como. The silk-worms, he told her, fed on the leaves of these trees. It was all part of a fascinating new world.

Jane's thoughts turned again to the clinic that they would soon reach and she determined to find out something about Duncan Frobisher from Mario. As the car sped across the plain she learned how Mario had first met Duncan Frobisher when they had worked together in the orthopaedic departmeint of a London teaching hospital. Duncan was considerably senior, but his inter-ested help had given rise to a friendship which on Mario's side obviously ap-proached hero worship. To him, Duncan Frobisher was the one factor that had enabled an unknown young Italian to make a small but significant name for himself in the field of orthopaedic medi-cine.

The car slowed gradually as they drove into the mountains and then began to climb steadily up the last steep gradient to the Villa Alto, high on the mountain-side. As the light began to fail and they neared the end of their journey Jane realised that she knew a great deal more about Mario Ronelli, but still very little about Duncan Frobisher or his clinic.

The Villa Alto was not a modern clinic but a converted villa, so it presented the appearance of a large family house to the eyes of approaching visitors. To Jane the villa looked dingy with its pink-brown walls, but she was soon to learn to value the restfulness of that colour to eyes strained by the strong sunlight on the masses of brilliant colour that make Italy so delightful to English eyes.

By the time they reached the clinic the light was fading fast and all the brilliance of the daytime scene was muted to a soft haze of almost indistinguishable shapes and colours.

As Mario led her under the portico to the main door a woman advanced from the shadowy hallway to greet them.

'Ah, here is Mary!' exclaimed Mario with pleasure. 'Mary, I've brought Miss Jane Marten to join us. I'll leave her with you and go to visit papa straight away.' With a gay bow to both he withdrew and left Jane to face her new life alone.

The woman with whom she had been left spoke for the first time as they turned towards the wide, sweeping staircase.

'I'm Mary Mackinlay, commonly known as Mac. I'm the general factotum enobled by the title of housekeeper.'

Jane knew that in Mac she had met another person whom she was definitely going to like during her stay at the Villa Alto. The Scotswoman led her up the staircase, pointing out the principal rooms as she went. At the end of a long corridor they stopped.

'And here is your room,' she announced, showing Jane into a large high-ceilinged room with tall double windows opening on to a balcony.

'Oh, but how lovely!' Jane exclaimed. 'A balcony all to myself! Is this really to be my room?' she asked, unbelievingly. Mary Mackinlay laughed.

'Well, there's a room at the back overlooking the kitchens if you'd prefer it. But I'd be grateful if you'd put up with this for tonight now that the bed's made up.' They laughed together and Jane knew that she had found a new friend.

When she was alone Jane decided to wash and change before looking at anything, but she had hardly opened her suitcase before there was a knock at the door. The visitor was a smiling Italian maid with a note from Dr Frobisher to say that he would see Miss Marten in the library.

The peremptory tone of this note aroused an unreasoning antagonism in Jane. Stubbornly quelling a schoolgirl impulse to obey his command at once, she thanked the maid who had brought the note. With deliberate attention to detail, she proceeded to unpack her first suitcase and shook out a suitable cotton dress before she started to wash and renew her light make-up. When she had stepped into the fresh yellow dress and fastened a wide belt round her waist she surveyed herself in the mirror of the dressing-table.

Her mood lightened as she felt the swirl of the full skirt about her legs, in delightful contrast to the restriction of the straight skirt of the suit that she had been wearing for so many hours. With a gay gesture she sprinkled some cologne from a travelling flask on her hands and smoothed them over her shining hair. This was the beginning of her new adventure and the dictatorial attitude of Max's brother was not going to spoil it for her.

Max had airily dismissed his brother as 'old Duncan', whom he described as a good sort but a bit on the serious side. It was with mixed feelings that Jane made her way down the wide staircase and across the marbled floor of the lofty hall to the open doors of a book-lined room which could only be the library to which she had been summoned.

As she stood in the doorway she became aware of the man standing in the half-light of an alcove. Her soft-soled sandals had obviously not warned him of her approach. For a moment she could watch him while he was still unaware of her presence.

Looking at the broad shoulders and the familiar set of the dark head, Jane experienced an excited thrill. She was loath to break the spell of that moment, but curious to know why Max should be in Italy so soon. The last time she had seen him he had spoken vaguely about seeing her in Italy in a couple of weeks or so, and that was only the evening before.

Drawing a deep breath to steady her voice, she allowed herself a short laugh that was meant to match his light-hearted mood as she stepped into the room.

'Hallo, stranger. This is a very pleasant surprise.'

Her voice was a little nervous and unsteady on the first words, but it quavered and failed completely as he turned to face her.

This man was indeed a stranger. In what subtle way his appearance differentiated him from Max she could not have described, except that what in Max was gay and charming was in this man translated into a disturbing quality of aloofness akin to arrogance. That Duncan Frobisher was not a man to be trifled with was something that Jane had already divined from his letters. What those letters had not prepared her for was his physical appearance. That this was Max's brother she had no doubt, the likeness was almost uncanny.

As Jane stood in the centre of the room, immobile in her confusion, she did not realise that her head lifted involuntarily, defying him to take advantage of her mistake. Her eyes flashed with anger at herself for the loss of her carefully prepared poise.

Duncan Frobisher returned her gaze steadily — if there was a glint of amusement in his eyes she could not see it in the dim light of the alcove where he was standing. His voice held no amusement as he spoke.

'Good evening, Miss Marten. I hope you do not always delay your actions until twenty minutes after they have become necessary.'

Jane was utterly unprepared for this complete dismissal of her mistake and she felt that he knew it. He had taken advantage of her confusion and her annoyance would not be contained.

'I hope that you do not always expect your staff to do without adequate time for a wash after a long journey, Dr Frobisher.' She knew that the retort was foolish and childish, but she had been goaded too far from her habitual calm to be reasonable.

A disconcertingly non-committal inclination of his head was her only answer until he had crossed the room in silence to stand by the open window. When he spoke again it was in the same impersonal tone that he had used for his first remark.

'Charming as the effect of your wash is, Miss Marten, I consider that you were more suitably dressed when you arrived. You will be able to unpack your uniform by the morning, I hope.'

The implication that he had watched her arrival was disconcerting enough, but his second remark left Jane speechless for a moment. She remembered the list of uniform that she had dismissed as being applicable only to nurses. With dangerous quiet she answered his implied question.

'I am not a nurse, Dr Frobisher.'

'Nevertheless the children have confidence in the uniform. If, as I understand, you have none, no doubt Mrs Mackinlay can find you something suitable until you can order your own.'

'That will not be necessary, thank you. I shall not be wearing uniform. I am a teacher, Dr Frobisher, not a nurse.' If Jane's calm held a dangerous undercurrent his was overriding.

'I am aware of that, Miss Marten, but the children are accustomed to the uniform.' He opened the door for her as he added with slight emphasis, 'You are here for the good of the children; not for a romantic interlude.'

Jane was about to speak when he cut her short once more. 'Goodnight, Miss Marten.'

The words were spoken with such inexorable finality that Jane found herself crossing the hallway again before her mind questioned the authority of his dismissal. Halting at the bottom of the staircase, she turned to retrace her steps and give battle. The doctor was still standing in the library doorway, in that moment looking so like Max that her resolution fled. Determined to retire if not triumphant at least undefeated, she met the steady regard of his grey eyes unflinchingly.

'Goodnight, Dr Frobisher.' It wasn't a very grand exit, but at least it was dignified.

The remark about a romantic interlude she was well aware was his way of acknowledging her mistake in taking him for Max. Worse, it told her that in that moment he had seen through her defensive exterior and for that she would find it hard to forgive him. She needed all the dignity she could muster to save her pride in the face of such unmasking.

As Jane turned to the staircase again Duncan Frobisher allowed himself a faint smile and firmly closed the library door. He had enough confidence in the reports he had received to believe that she was an excellent teacher, but that Jane Marten was any different from other women in her human relationships he was not prepared to believe. Like any other woman, she would be incapable of maintaining an impersonal relationship with anyone. Duncan Frobisher had worked with women for too long to be unaware of their weaknesses. To him they were necessary encumbrances that must be borne with so that he could carry out his work efficiently.

Jane's anger was boiling by the time she reached her room. Shutting the door with a satisfactory bang, she relieved her feelings by letting forth a vivid description of just how pompous, priggish and dictatorial she considered Dr Duncan Frobisher.

'Well, at least you must admit that he's been poured into a perfect masculine mould,' remarked an amused voice.

For the first time Jane looked across the room and saw that Mary Mackinlay was seated in the chair by the window. She felt that one more such happening would make her scream with rage. Mac laughed good-naturedly.

'Don't mind me,' she said. 'And, incidentally, don't mind Duncan too much. You've obviously started off on the wrong foot with him, but your description doesn't really fit at all when you know him.'

Jane collapsed into the opposite

chair. 'Would you mind answering one simple question?' she asked. 'Just how much say does he have here?'

'Simple answer to a simple question, he has the last word in everything.'

'That's what I was afraid of,' sighed Jane. 'Where does his brother fit in then?'

'Max? He doesn't. He has a sort of high society practice in Milan. Though he does spend a lot of time here, when he can.'

'Oh.' The sound that escaped Jane's lips was no more than an involuntary recognition of the other's words. This was news that she was completely unprepared for. She had never considered the possibility that Max's work was at any place other than the clinic.

Mary Mackinlay's words broke into her thoughts. 'If you knew Max you wouldn't need to ask what say he has with Duncan.'

'I do know Max,' said Jane succinctly.

'Oh.' It was Mac's turn to be at a loss for words, but not for long. 'Well, you must see what I mean then. They are as alike as most twins in many ways, but when they do differ they do it with a vengeance.'

So that was the explanation of the uncanny likeness: Duncan and Max were twin brothers. Reluctantly Jane had to admit to herself that she did see exactly. All Max's gaiety and charm, endearing qualities though they were, would be no match for his brother's unrelenting strength of purpose.

Mac watched the changing expressions on the younger girl's face and when she spoke again it was with sympathetic concern. 'You poor child. He really has got you down tonight, hasn't he? Well, I'll leave you now to get a good long sleep. We can talk in the morning. Have you everything for tonight?'

'Yes, thank you,' replied Jane. 'And . . . please forgive my outburst.'

Mac's answer was a soft laugh. 'You'll find the place is clean and the food is good anyway,' she said. 'And if it isn't I'll be knowing the reason why.

Goodnight now, and don't let that fine figure of a man spoil your night's rest.'

As she got ready for bed Jane thought gratefully that at least she should be sure of sympathetic companionship from Mary Mackinlay.

Lying in bed she could watch the stars in the velvet sky. In their remoteness they had a lot in common with Duncan Frobisher, Jane reflected.

When she woke to the brilliant sunlight of her first morning in Italy Jane mentally reviewed her first encounter with her new employer. Reluctant though she was to admit it, she knew that he was right in saying that the children would accept her more readily if she wore the uniform that they were used to. Accordingly she sought out Mac at the first opportunity and managed to build up a passably well-fitting uniform from those in the store-room.

At breakfast in the large refectory she was introduced to the nursing staff that consisted of an English matron, two other English girls, and a seemingly indefinite number of Italian girls of various ranks which Jane could not begin to sort out. The matron was another cheerful woman who was obviously on terms of great friendship with Mary Mackinlay. Together they introduced Jane to the rest of the nursing staff. Apart from the fact that Dorothy Archer was a chubby redhead and Christine Powell a somewhat distant blonde, Jane retained no lasting impression of her introduction to the two English nurses.

The working day began immediately after breakfast, without the appearance of Duncan Frobisher. It was not for some time that Jane learned that he used the quiet hours of the early part of the day for his routine office work. The major part of the day he spent among the children unless there was any surgery to keep him in the operating theatre. His secretary being on holiday kept him in his office more than usual during Jane's first fortnight at the clinic.

As the matron led a tour of the various departments there were many questions for Jane to ask.

'We have some children who are bedridden,' Matron told her, 'but most of them don't come to us until they are convalescent.'

'And where do the children come from?' Jane asked, listening to the babel of shrill voices. 'They're not all English, are they?'

'Good gracious, no. Very few in fact. Most of them are Italian, Swiss or Austrian. Signore Ronelli is very insistent that the clinic should be open to all nationalities.'

'Signore Ronelli?' Jane queried.

'Yes, didn't you know about him?' Matron was obviously surprised.

'I know nothing except about the numbers of children and staff and my own duties. Is this Signore Ronelli related to Dr Mario Ronelli?'

'Yes, indeed. Dr Ronelli is the old man's son. They are just about the wealthiest Italians about here. You must have heard about the famous Ronelli jewels.'

Jane did vaguely remember having read about the fabulous jewel collection and wondered why she hadn't recalled it when Mario mentioned his name. 'So, it is the Ronelli family that actually owns the clinic?' she asked.

Matron was obviously a little embarrassed at having started to discuss the subject and finding it difficult to know where to stop. Reluctant as she was, Jane gradually drew from her the story of how the family had given over their villa and a considerable sum of money to a trust to run the clinic. Apparently old Signore Ronelli had first met Duncan Frobisher when Mario was still a student. The older man had come to value Duncan so highly that he had insisted that his cherished idea for this clinic could only be brought to life by a man such as Duncan Frobisher. So it was that Duncan had joined the Ronelli family in Italy; Duncan was a member of the trust which administered the

clinic as well as its medical superintendent.

All this Jane learned bit by bit as
she followed Matron through long
corridors and rooms which had been
converted into wards and nurseries.
Two of the more spacious rooms were
given over to a gymnasium and a
magnificently equipped operating theatre. Another surprise was to learn that
all this was not only available to the
children of wealthy parents as Jane had
supposed. The trust fund made it
possible for children from very humble
homes to have treatment at the Villa
Alto if they were transferred from a
hospital for special care.

Jane had not come across such
philanthropy before and she was curious to meet Signore Cosimo Ronelli.
Mario's father must be an extraordinary man, she thought.

When they finally returned to the
central hallway Matron knocked on
the library door and Jane once again
found herself face to face with her

enigmatic employer. No, she must correct that thought now that she knew about Mario Ronelli and his father.

Duncan Frobisher was seated with his back to the long open windows, obviously busy with a considerable amount of paper work. As Jane and Matron entered the room he rose and, merely glancing at Jane, turned to smile at her companion.

'Good morning, Matron. I've just been struggling with these reports. I must admit I'll be glad to have a secretary again next week. Good morning, Miss Marten. I hope you have settled down as well as possible under the circumstances.'

The double-edged remark did not miss Jane's alert defence. 'Perfectly well, thank you.' Her chin lifted as she spoke and she found her eyes caught again by the cool appraising glance of Max's brother. She was sure that she would have to keep herself from actively disliking this man. Unreasonable pride forbade her to avoid his glance even while it disconcerted her to a degree that she would not have believed possible.

Matron unwittingly saved the situation by saying something about seeing Dr Frobisher later and withdrawing. Hardly had the door closed, however, before another salvo was fired broadside at Jane's self-esteem.

'I see that we shall easily find ourselves in agreement on some matters at least, Miss Marten.'

Seeing that his glance indicated her uniform, Jane blushed with indignation. Why, she demanded of herself, had she allowed him to gain this moral victory so early?

No man had ever before affected her as Duncan Frobisher could. He had the facility for stripping her of all the carefully acquired poise of the careerist and then pointedly ignoring the woman he had revealed. Jane, in common with many career women, was defensive about her relationship with men in her working life; but she knew, to her own irritation, that a little attention to her femininity would have averted the anger of her bruised pride. This knowledge only served to increase her defensive attitude on the first morning in her new job.

Duncan Frobisher believed that women who worked with men were entitled to exactly the same consideration as their male colleagues. He was a man perfectly at ease in the confidence that he could do his job well; he spoke to his colleagues when he had something to say to them about their work, but otherwise saved his breath and conserved his mental energy. This taciturn attitude was incomprehensible to most of the women with whom he came in contact, and Jane was no exception. To her, conversation was necessary to maintain mental contact between two people and silence could only mean displeasure or boredom.

The silence that followed Matron's departure was a disturbed one for Jane, and the disturbance was only enhanced by the extraordinary likeness between the two Frobisher brothers. She was used to finding that handsome men were impossibly vain. In fact only a few days before she had taunted Max for that very fault. Looking now at the brother who was undoubtedly more handsome in every detail of his fine tanned features, Jane knew that she had met a man who could never be taxed with physical vanity. He was quite unaware of his looks, and that was more than could be said for Max, Jane conceded grudgingly. She knew in her heart that Duncan Frobisher was as fine a man as his appearance would suggest and for that very reason she found herself ready to pounce on his slightest fault, to magnify it and excuse her unreasonable antagonism.

The interview that followed was restrained and businesslike. After a short summary of the case of each of the six children who were to be her special charges, they went together to the nursery to meet Jane's new pupils. It had been agreed that Jane should teach all the deaf children together as they were all English except for two little Swiss boys whose parents both spoke English.

The morning passed quickly as Jane made her plans. She was amazed to find how readily all her requirements were met, and all obstacles to her plans carefully rearranged to allow the children plenty of time for other treatment without interfering with her lessons.

* * *

The weeks that followed were so full that Jane woke one morning to find that she had been at the Villa Alto for a month.

There was still no news of Max and she was very diffident about approaching anyone on the subject. The uncertainy of his arrival was disturbing her usual calm. Jane knew it was the source of many of her increasingly frequent disagreements with Duncan Frobisher.

In an effort to dispel the dejection which hung over her, as each successive post brought no letter from Max, Jane planned to spend an afternoon exploring the district around the Villa Alto.

On the morning of her proposed expedition she had yet another disagreement with Duncan Frobisher. She was sitting with her class and little David Ives was on her lap. She had been told less than usual about David's past and his clinical notes only showed that he had been involved in a car crash in which his mother had been killed and he severely injured. His injuries had healed more slowly than they should have done in a healthy four-year-old. The broken leg responded well enough to treatment at first, but David had seemed unable, or unwilling, to bring it back into full movement. Under patient physiotherapy at the Villa Alto the range of movement had been gradually restored until, by the time that Jane arrived at the clinic, there was little trace of physical injury.

Thus far David's recovery was satisfactory, but the accident had so shocked the child that he had apparently lost all his power of speech. So, although he was not deaf, David had joined Jane's class.

Jane had already become very fond of the dark-haired little imp of mischief. She told herself that it was because of his very special circumstances that she was particularly interested in David, but in her more honest moments she knew that the child had found a place in her heart. It was her self-condemnation on this score that made her resentful and defensive when Duncan Frobisher taxed her with giving overmuch attention to this one child.

As children will, the whole class, which had been so absorbed in her teaching a minute before, broke into a disorderly mob as Duncan Frobisher entered the classroom. They adored him on sight in the inexplicable way of the very young and always rushed to him. All, on that occasion, except young David, who sat firmly on Jane's lap and only spared a glance for his erstwhile idol before he turned worshipping eyes back to Jane's face.

The incident might have passed unnoticed if Jane had been quick to move, but as it was, she found herself sitting in obvious isolation with David on her knee; the pair of them suffering the undisguised displeasure of the medical superintendent.

Later in the morning Jane found herself in the library trying to find a reasonable answer to a very reasonable question from her employer.

'I should like to know, Miss Marten, why it is that you give so much time and attention to David Ives in particular.' The silence that followed was almost tangible. 'Well, Miss Marten; I am waiting for your explanation. You may well have a very good reason for what you are doing. On the other hand, you may be allowing sentiment to affect your work. In that case I should point out that I cannot allow such behaviour in this clinic.'

He had unwisely raised a point which Jane could use to base her answer on. 'Do you not consider that to give a little affection to a child who will never know his mother's love is part of my work, Dr Frobisher?'

His gaze held hers as she spoke and his expression, though as inscrutable as ever, left her feeling that he was looking into her very soul for the answer to an unasked question. It was a very uncomfortable experience. When he spoke again, it was in his usual impersonal enigmatic tone.

'If I could believe that you were acting in a completely rational manner and solely for the good of your patient, Miss Marten, I should agree with you whole-heartedly.'

Jane could hardly suppress a smile at the thought of Duncan Frobisher doing anything in such a manner. To act wholeheartedly, to Jane, meant to feel and to show enthusiasm. She had never seen Dr Frobisher show enthusiasm for anything other than the impersonal details of the organisation of the routine of the clinic. If he was wholehearted in anything, thought Jane, it was in his belief in his own self-sufficiency; she was tempted to wish that his heart was a little less whole in that respect so that he might appear at least a little more human.

'I hardly think that David can suffer from the limited amount of attention that I can give him,' she remarked with asperity.

'That is exactly my point, Miss Marten,' was the reply. 'Your time with the children is strictly limited and the singling out of any child for particular attention can only lead to a corresponding lack of attention for the others.'

'And my point, Dr Frobisher, is that alone out of all the children David has no mother. These children are all very young, but they are all aware of the security which their parents' love gives them. I believe that the lack of this security is as important a factor in David's lack of speech as the result of his accident.'

Duncan Frobisher's expression was to remain in Jane's mind for a long time. She saw in his face for a fleeting moment such inexpressable hurt that her one impulse was to rush to offer womanly comfort. As he turned away from her, she watched the broad back that was so like Max's; turbulent emotions fought for her own power of speech. She did not know whether she wanted to cry or to laugh — to cry for this man who had, for a brief moment, shown her that he had a heart, or to laugh at her own ridiculous reaction to the revelation.

If Jane had experienced any doubt as to what her action should be, the tone of Duncan Frobisher's voice as he answered her last remark would have removed that doubt for ever.

'Thank you, Miss Marten. I asked you why you give so much time and attention to this child. You have explained your motive and expressed your opinion. We shall let the matter rest for the time being.'

The dismissal was obvious and Jane felt that no reply was needed apart from a murmured 'Thank you, Dr Frobisher.' Though what on earth she had to thank him for she could not imagine. With her hand on the door, she was recalled for a moment as he added —

'And Miss Marten, please remember that the cases of the other children also have 'factors' to quote yourself; factors equally worthy of your attention.'

In the hall outside, with the door closed between herself and the library, Jane realised that the parting remark had been delivered with a smile.

It was the first time that she had seen Duncan Frobisher smile at anyone but the children. The experience was not altogether as pleasing as it might have been. The enigmatic doctor was easily classified, but this smiling edition was a disturbingly unknown quantity.

In all fairness Jane had to admit to herself that she had not exactly helped Duncan Frobisher to be pleasant to her during these past weeks. His very likeness to Max had been a source of continual irritation to her. With a mental shake she reminded herself that the rest of the day was her own. The affairs of the clinic were to be forgotten for a few hours while she enjoyed her first intimate sight of the area that was to be her home for the next few months at least. 'If I don't drive the Great Man to distraction before that,' she told herself.

By the evening Jane was happy to be able to make her way to a secluded corner of the garden and start her weekly letter to her parents. As she sat on the stone seat, the gentle evening warmth seeped through her body and the heady mixture of scents from the flowering shrubs lulled her senses until she sat immobile, her letter forgotten, just absorbing the seductive beauty of her surroundings.

She was startled out of her daydream by voices which came clearly to her as she sat concealed, a few yards from the speakers on the other side of the shrubbery. Duncan Frobisher's voice sounded clearly in the still evening air. The second, lighter-toned voice was unmistakably Max's. Jane had long since ceased to expect his arrival with each new day so that his presence on this beautiful evening came with the delightful surprise of an unexpected gift.

Now, as she listened to the voices of the brothers discussing various aspects of the administration of the clinic, she was amused to realise that the seemingly light-hearted Max was as enthusiastic as his brother about their work. He was questioning Duncan minutely about the condition of the various children; as Jane listened, she became aware that his air of gay confidence was rooted, not in irresponsibility, but in an unusually clear-minded understanding of every aspect of his own particular field of medicine. It became increasingly obvious that each brother had a high regard for the opinion of the other.

The two men slowly rounded the end of the shrubbery and came fully into Jane's field of vision. For the first time she saw them side by side and once again marvelled at their likeness. As she watched Max closely for the moment when he would first see her, she became aware of an acute sense of disappointment, strangely mingled with an inexplicable feeling of relief. For all the similarities between the brothers, there was a fundamental difference which was sharply emphasized as they stood together.

It was Duncan Frobisher who first noticed Jane's presence.

'Good evening, Miss Marten,' he greeted her, formally.

Max was his usual informal self and was soon teasing Jane about her uniform, which she had put on when she made a quick visit to the children just before coming out to write her letter. It hadn't seemed worth changing yet again that day.

3

'Why, Jane!' he exclaimed. 'Whatever prompted you to hide your pretty form under this disguise?' As he spoke, he turned her round by the shoulder to get a better view of garb that she had so quickly come to take for granted.

It was Duncan Frobisher who saved her from answering the question.

'Miss Marten agreed with me that the children would accept her more readily if she wore the uniform,' he announced firmly.

Jane felt an insane desire to giggle at this crisp description of the battle of wills that had ended in her wearing the uniform much against her own wishes. An impish smile reached her lips, but she refrained from comment out of respect for Duncan Frobisher's senior position. His brother had no such inhibitions and burst out laughing.

'Well Jane, you've certainly let me down this time. I thought that you would be able to stand up to this overbearing monster better than that.'

Their eyes met in mutual amusement, but Jane's reply was suitably grave.

'As Dr Frobisher says, I agreed with him.' Suddenly she was annoyed that Max should force her into this position in front of his brother.

'Like heck you did,' agreed the irrepressible Max. 'If I know Duncan, he said 'wear it' and you did. Though why you should submit to such despotism, I can't imagine.'

Jane found it difficult to answer this without embarrassment, but once again Duncan Frobisher intercepted her reply.

'Perhaps Miss Marten is better aware of the value of discipline than you imagine,' he remarked, with an air suggesting that the subject should be dismissed, which was not lost on his audience.

'Maybe,' agreed Max lightly. 'But Miss Marten is not always Miss Marten. Did you know, Duncan, that her name is

Jane, that she looks a dream when she wears pale green and that she dances a waltz that is an absolute poem of movement?'

Jane flushed crimson at such personal reminiscences, but Duncan remained imperturbably distant. 'Indeed?' was his sole reply to his brother's exuberant revelations.

As they were parting, Max made a mock-latin bow and planted a kiss firmly on her hand before she was aware of his intention. Although she avoided Duncan Frobisher's glance, Jane was conscious that his grey eyes had not missed one detail of the gesture. The knowledge left her strangely disturbed.

The two men passed out of sight across the terrace, but Jane could not settle again to write her letter. The feeling of disappointment that had come to her on first seeing Max with his brother had grown stronger as they spoke, until now she was thoroughly bemused by her own emotions. Her pleasure at seeing Max again was nothing like the excitement that she had anticipated during the past weeks. She recalled vividly the moment when she first saw the brothers side by side. Max appeared as no more than the delightful sketch on which a great artist had based the richly coloured oil portrait that was Duncan. Reluctantly Jane had to admit, if only to her inner self, that charming and delightful as Max might be, it was Duncan Frobisher who had the depth and strength of character which commanded admiration and respect.

As she sat and pondered over the contrasting characters of the two brothers, she considered the possibility that her interest in Max might be nothing more than escapism; a bridge from the old life to the new. Otherwise could she quietly sit here and dissect his character as she was doing, much less compare him unfavourably with anyone as remote from herself as Duncan Frobisher?

It was Mario Ronelli who brought her thoughts back to the present as he rounded the corner of the shrubbery and came towards her.

'Ah, Jane, I have been looking for you. But why is a beautiful girl like you sitting alone on such a lovely evening?'

Jane smiled up at him and thought how well he filled the role of the romantic latin hero as he stood looking down at her in the soft sunlight of the early evening.

'I was indulging in the luxury of being alone with my thoughts, Mario,' she replied laughingly.

His darkly handsome face was grave with concern and it was plain to her that his latin soul could not comprehend her wish to be alone.

'But that is so wrong,' he protested. 'One so young should be with others to dance and to be gay.'

Jane moved across the seat, inviting him to sit beside her, but — in the true romantic tradition — he preferred to lean on the back of the seat so that he was looking down at her as he spoke. She laughed up at him. As always, she was happily relaxed in his company.

'And now tell me why you were

looking for me, Mario,' she suggested.

'I wanted to ask you to come to a little party at my father's house. My sister is coming home from Rome and we shall give a small party of welcome.'

Jane was touched by the suggestion that she should join this family reunion.

'Why Mario, that is very kind of you. But your sister doesn't even know me, and she will want to meet her own friends first when she gets home.'

'But no,' Mario's tone was firm. 'I have told Teresa much about you and it is she who says that you must come to the party.'

'In that case, Mario, I'll be delighted to come.' Jane was both amused and pleased that Teresa Ronelli had already heard of her from Mario.

They talked together for a while; Mario telling her about the history of the villa and the gardens, and about the exploits of previous generations of the Ronelli family. Jane loved to listen to him describing people and events from the past so vividly in soft broken

English. Only the cool evening air, reminding her of the need for a jacket, made them move at last and cross the terrace to the villa. As they walked, Mario once again referred to the coming party and to his sister. It appeared that Teresa had been studying singing in Rome for the past two years. As they reached the door which led into the main hallway, Mario placed a detaining hand on Jane's arm. His eyes were dancing with fun as she turned to him in enquiry.

'I wish to share a secret with you,' he said. 'My father hopes that this will be a special party for Teresa. He hopes to announce her betrothal.'

'How exciting, Mario,' exclaimed Jane delightedly. 'An engagement is always such fun.'

'Such fun.' Mario mocked her accent. 'You English have no romance in your language. You hear of a betrothal and you say 'such fun'. I am not sure that it will be good for my poor Teresa to marry an Englishman, even if he is an admirable doctor.'

Jane gazed at him in astonishment for a stunned moment.

'Do you mean that your sister is going to marry Dr Frobisher?' Her voice was low and not quite steady as she asked the question.

'It is not arranged,' Mario replied. 'But my father has always hoped that it would be so when Teresa was ready for marriage. So now, you see, we hope for the betrothal.'

'I see.' Jane's voice was oddly flat and toneless to her own ears. 'Thank you, Mario, for letting me share your secret.'

'And remember, Jane, that it is still a secret for a short time,' he said. 'Good night.' He smiled as he bowed over her hand, turned quickly, and left her.

Jane suddenly felt very cold although the evening air was still warm in the shelter of the villa. She too turned quickly, to seek the privacy of her own room. As she felt the door close behind her and knew that she was alone, her limbs began to tremble violently.

Mario's words had opened Jane's

eyes to something that she found almost impossible to believe. He had shown her, with unintentionally cruel clarity, exactly why she no longer thrilled to the sound of Max's voice or to his nearness; shown her too the reason for her strangely unsettled happiness in the past few weeks, which she had attributed to the continual anticipation of Max's arrival. Suddenly and clearly she knew that it was neither Max's charm nor Mario's gallantry that had disturbed her usually calm view of life. 'But you don't lose your grip over a man to whom you've hardly spoken two social words,' Jane told herself firmly. Deliberately she kept her mind blank as she crossed the room and splashed her burning face with comfortingly cool water. Only a few moments ago she had been so cold. This could not happen! Of all the men she had ever met in her busy career she had to fall with adolescent abandon into an overwhelming sea of infatuation for Duncan Frobisher.

Well, at any rate, Jane told herself, it could only be infatuation for a man she knew so little of; and that was something that burned itself out. She must come to grips with herself and wait for this wild, ridiculous feeling to die a natural death. After all, the job would only last until the present group of children were well enough to return to their own homes.

A few days later a printed invitation from Signore Cosimo Ronelli, requesting the pleasure of her company at a party to celebrate the homecoming of his daughter, was a sharp reminder of recent happenings. Jane showed the invitation to Mac as they sat together on her little balcony in the evening sunlight.

'Is Teresa Ronelli younger or older than Mario?' she asked.

'Teresa? She's four years younger than Mario, but he's older than you would think and she is very mature, and very Italian.'

'Mario says that she has been

studying singing in Rome.' Jane chose her words carefully. 'Does that mean that she wants to make a career of singing, or is it just for her own pleasure?'

'My dear Jane!' Mac laughed delightedly. 'You just must not say things like that when the Ronellis are listening. In Italy one *studies* music even if one is a successful operatic singer. Teresa has already achieved considerable fame. Her teachers think that she could rank among the great sopranos,' Mac gazed absently out over the lovely mountain view as she added — 'But I don't think she will somehow.'

'What makes you say that?' The words were spoken casually enough but Jane's whole body was curiously tense as she waited for the reply.

'It's difficult to say.' Mac spoke thoughtfully. 'Teresa is too real a person. She is too gentle and warm-hearted for that kind of life. I think that when she falls in love she will put that first. Of course, I may be quite wrong, but I'm usually right about that sort of thing.'

Every word that Mac spoke was building up a more formidable picture to Jane. At first she had thought of Teresa Ronelli as little more than a schoolgirl, then for a brief moment she had clung to the idea of a singer passionately devoted to her art, but Mac's words had drawn a picture of an artist who was also a warm-hearted woman.

Mac continued speaking.

'You know, Jane, I think you and Teresa will find a great deal in common. She speaks very good English and always wants to practise it on new people.'

Jane was saved from having to find a suitable answering remark because Mac was called away at that moment. Left sitting alone on her romantic balcony, Jane looked down to the beautiful lake below and smiled a little wanly to herself. Here she was, in a situation that would be the dream of many a girl's life and she had to fall in love with the most unattainable man whom she had ever had the misfortune to meet. She already knew Duncan Frobisher too well to believe that he would give anyone reason to expect him to act in a particular way unless he had already decided to do so. And wasn't it inevitable that such a man should find attraction in a woman who was a superbly finished example of her sex such as Mac's words suggested Teresa Ronelli to be?

The days continued to slip by uneventfully and Jane gradually learned to steel herself against the impact of frequent meetings with Duncan Frobisher. It was a great relief that he lived very much on his own and rarely joined the staff at meals or during the evenings. Lulled by the security of routine, Jane found an uneasy peace until the evening when she received a note to say that Duncan wished to speak to her in the library at once. The note was in his usual peremptory style. As she hurried to comply with the request, she recalled the first such note which she had received and the subsequent interview.

She found him seated at his desk.

'Oh Miss Marten, please sit down for a minute.'

He continued writing while Jane sat watching him; outwardly calm but inwardly indignant that he should send for her so urgently and then completely ignore her presence. When at last he spoke it was without raising his head.

'Are you happy with us, Miss Marten?' The question was so sudden and unexpected that she could not completely control her voice as she replied.

'Yes. Yes thank you, Dr Frobisher, I am very happy.'

His acknowledgement of her reply was no more than a non-committal grunt. He collected the papers on the desk and methodically piled them onto a tray before another word was spoken. Jane wondered if she would ever become accustomed to his economy of words; she was uncomfortably aware of the silence that lay between them in the great book-lined room while pale sunlight played on the carpet in dappled patterns.

Like most women Jane was ill at ease in a silence that held no communicating point of sympathy. She longed to speak, to say anything to break the tension that was mounting within herself, but she knew too well by now that with Duncan Frobisher she must wait until he was prepared to continue speaking.

At last he looked across the desk at her and, despite all her determination to remain businesslike, a tingling sense of excitement gripped her as their eyes met for a moment. Duncan indulged in one of his rare smiles as he spoke.

'I haven't had much opportunity to discuss your work since you joined us here, Miss Marten.' His hands wandered through his pockets, slowly collecting all the paraphernalia of the pipe-smoker. Jane thought that she had never seen him so relaxed and socially inclined before. She hardly heard his words as she listened to the deep undertones of his quiet voice.

'I hope,' he was saying, 'that you are not suffering from too many problems.'

The pause which followed seemed to invite her contribution. With a supreme effort of will she brought her mind back to the subject under discussion.

'No. I don't think that there are any serious problems at present.'

'Good. I certainly congratulate you on the progress of your pupils. I would like some reports from you though. If you will write me an individual report for each one we can then spend a while discussing them as soon as possible.'

As always when her work was under discussion all self-consciousness left Jane. Her answer was ready and spontaneous.

'I should be pleased to be able to do that. In fact I always make out weekly reports for my own information. I can send you copies of them very soon.'

Her answer obviously pleased Duncan, though his only indication was a muttered 'Good' as he commenced to fill his pipe. The motions were so familiar that Jane had a hard fight to quell disturbing emotions as she watched the movements of his hands. The silence continued while he leaned back in his chair and drew quietly on the pipe until it burned to his satisfaction.

'And now, Miss Marten, I am driving to Milan next Tuesday to spend a day at a medical conference. As Dr Hamilton-Ayres of London is reading a paper on the instruction of deaf children in the same session, I thought that you might like to join me for the day.'

Jane took a deep uncertain breath before replying to the implied question.

'Thank you very much, Dr Frobisher. I should certainly like to hear Dr Hamilton-Ayres.'

As she spoke their eyes met and held. For a moment she could have believed that his eyes were full of the laughter that she associated with Max in a teasing mood. But even as she spoke the laughter seemed to die and to be replaced by that same enigmatic look, so akin to anger, that she had seen before. When he spoke his voice was once again expressionless and impersonal.

'Very well. That's decided. I shall be ready to leave at eight o'clock on Tuesday morning. Please make your own arrangements accordingly.'

As usual Duncan had concluded the interview and given her the cue for departure.

4

On the day before the Milan conference Jane found concentration difficult. By the evening she felt mentally exhausted and yet she still had a lot of work to do in order to leave the following day absolutely free. In the early evening she decided to take her books and notes to the secluded corner of the shrubbery that had become a favourite retreat for her. As she crossed the terrace she saw Mario walking towards the villa and with him a small, dark woman who moved with the intriguing grace peculiar to latin women. Mario waved gaily and Jane reluctantly turned her steps from the seclusion of the shrubbery towards the advancing couple. Mario's handsome young face was alight with pleasure as they met.

'So our English flower was looking for her natural shade again,' he teased.

'You must learn to flower boldly in the sun, Jane.'

Jane, as usual, felt a lightening of her mood in his presence. The laughter with which she answered his greeting was happy and spontaneous. Mario placed a hand below the elbow of the dark girl who was standing quietly beside him and drew her towards Jane.

'And here is my sister Teresa,' he announced, with a note of pride.

So this was Teresa Ronelli. Jane had expected more statuesque proportions — an altogether different kind of person. The almost fragile beauty of this girl was something completely unexpected. She was breathtaking in her almost miniature perfection.

'I am so very pleased to meet you, Miss Marten.'

Her English pronunciation was excellent and her voice full and unexpectedly rich for one so small.

'I have heard so much about you, Signorina.'

Jane suddenly felt very conscious of

her own voice in comparison, but in spite of her own feeling of inadequacy she instinctively liked the beautiful Italian girl. They talked conventionally for a few minutes before Mario took his sister's arm with a proprietorial air.

'We must now go in to find Duncan,' he reminded her. 'He will be waiting to see you, Teresa.'

They parted with promises to meet again soon and Jane made her way to the shelter of the shrubbery. Once seated among the flowering shrubs and gazing across to the mountain peaks, Jane let her thoughts run riot. If concentration had been difficult before, it was now impossible. The disturbing meeting with Mario's lovely sister had broken down all the carefully erected emotional barriers that Jane had used for protection during the past days.

She sat until the sun went down, without opening a book or writing a single word; just willing herself to accept the beauty of Teresa as the natural and inevitable complement to the distinguished handsomeness of Duncan Frobisher. It was madness to be so affected by a man whom she had known for only a few short weeks, she told herself fiercely. And yet she knew now that from the first moment when she had seen him her life had been changed. All the minor battles which they had fought in the early days were, she knew, brought about by her own attitude. They had supplied an almost instinctive camouflage for her true feelings. How she was to go on for weeks or even months in this atmosphere she did not know. It would have been easy enough in England to avoid meeting him or even to change her job, but here where they lived under the same roof meetings were inevitable.

With a sigh Jane began to gather her books when she suddenly recalled the reason for her need to work that evening. The ordeal of a complete day in Duncan's company was still ahead of her.

In spite of a restless night, Jane was

awake early and waiting in the main hall when Duncan Frobisher appeared punctually on the stroke of eight o'clock. With no more acknowledgement of her presence than a conventional 'Good morning', he led the way to the waiting car.

The first part of the journey was accomplished in unrelenting silence, but as they left the clinic further behind them he began to comment on the countryside. As they passed through little-known towns and less-known villages he showed himself to be surprisingly well-informed about the agriculture and industry of the area. Jane was blissfully content to sit beside him and watch the passing scene as they drove southward across the plain. In his present communicative mood, Duncan Frobisher was a very pleasant companion.

Sooner than she would have believed possible they were passing the Arch of Peace and Jane was entering Milan for the second time. They drove straight to the great house that had been put at the disposal of the medical conference.

Together they walked up the broad steps to the main doorway. Before she stepped out of the sunlight, Jane could not resist the urge to turn and gaze for a few moments at the street below. The strange mixture of the spirit of a modern industrial town and a city of beautiful and ancient buildings excited her romantic sense. She received a vivid impression of rich, uneven colour. This she felt was more truly Italy than the serene beauty of the alpine lakes.

For a few minutes she quite forgot Duncan Frobisher by her side as she stood watching the scene below. His hand on her arm recalled her thoughts with a rush as she turned to him. He was smiling at her, with none of the irony that she had come to associate with his attitude to anything that was not directly associated with his work. When he spoke it was in the gentle voice that he rarely used to anyone but the children.

'Poor Jane. You have just discovered Italy and you are doomed to spend the day in a stuffy conference room.'

The hand on her arm guided her through the doorway into a shadowy, marbled hall. After the brilliance of the sunlit scene outside it was impossible to see anything of the interior of the building at first. However, Jane was in no mood to appreciate architectural beauties even when her eyes became accustomed to the dim light.

'Poor Jane,' he had said. Poor Jane, indeed! The fact that he had called her by her name for the first time brought little pleasure. From Max or Mario such teasing would have amused her, but not from Duncan. He was treating her as he would one of the children. Kindness, tolerance and gentle discipline! How often she had heard him state his belief in these qualities. Now she was being treated to a dose of the medicine as prescribed.

Jane smiled wryly. Here she was, being escorted by a man who drew admiring glances from women wherever he went, and he was treating her with exactly the same attentive consideration that he would have shown to any of the children in his care. Seething with indignation, which was none the less real because it was unjustifiable, she followed his tall, striding form into the conference hall where the meeting was just opening. All conversation was quickly hushed as the speakers took their places on the raised platform. The main speaker was a man who she knew well from her training days. Jane soon ceased to be aware of the disturbing presence of Duncan Frobisher seated beside her.

At the end of the morning he left her with a murmured apology before he made his way through the departing crowd to intercept a man whom he wished to speak to.

The lecture by her old tutor, Dr Hamilton-Ayres, had had a soothing influence on Jane's ruffled nerves. Sternly she told herself that she had no right to expect anything but formal courtesy from the man who was already as good as engaged to Teresa Ronelli. As she stood waiting for Duncan Frobisher and looking at a particularly lovely representation of the Madonna, she heard her name called and turned to see Dr Hamilton-Ayres crossing the room towards her.

'Miss Marten,' he greeted her. 'I recognised you earlier and I was afraid I'd missed you at the end of the meeting. What brings you among a crowd of stuffy old medical men?'

'I came to hear you read your paper, Doctor, and I'd like to thank you for a very interesting meeting.'

In reply to his question Jane explained how she came to be in Italy and found that the older man knew Duncan Frobisher well.

'What I'd like to know is what keeps that young man out here,' the old doctor muttered gruffly. 'That small clinic was all very fine for early experience, but he should be moving on by now.'

This was a point of view which Jane had not considered before, and although she knew that the words were more thoughts spoken aloud than specifically addressed to her, she found them interesting.

'Perhaps Dr Frobisher prefers to work with small numbers of patients and to know them individually,' she suggested tentatively.

'Hmm!' the old teacher grunted, disbelievingly. 'He's likely to find himself stuck in this backwater. Wouldn't have thought it of him.' Again he was talking more to himself than to Jane. 'Too good to vegetate; brilliant mind, though I abhor the expression. He'll regret it. Mark my words — he'll regret it.'

Jane was amused to notice that the clever old doctor had not changed at all since her own student days. His habit of predicting disaster in every situation had given rise to many disrespectful jokes among his students. Nevertheless his classes had always been fired by the old man's enthusiasm for his subject. Noticing that Jane had not replied to his prediction on Duncan Frobisher's future, the doctor turned his attention to her.

'And what about you, young woman. Do you intend to stick in this backwater with him? Eh!'

'My work at the clinic is only temporary,' Jane tried hard to suppress a smile as he continued.

'Very glad to hear it. Very glad indeed, my dear.' He was apparently unaware of the quiet return of Duncan who now stood a little apart waiting for the conversation to end. To Jane's acute embarrassment he could hardly fail to overhear the next remarks delivered in the old doctor's penetrating tones. 'And now don't you go getting yourself involved, young woman. Frobisher is a nice enough fellow I grant you, but if he intends to spend his life in that tin-pot clinic of his, he's a fool. You come home when your work is finished. Come and see me. I'll fix you up. You come home and marry some sensible chap, if you must marry at all.'

Knowing the old man as she did, Jane would normally have laughed off such remarks from him without a moment's thought. Among his favourite calamities, the marriage of his women students always held pride of place. With Duncan Frobisher standing by it was not so easy to laugh off the situation. The interpretation that could be put on the remarks of the doctor by a casual listener was too embarrassing to allow a light-hearted dismissal of the subject. It was Duncan himself who saved Jane from the necessity to answer the older man's remarks as he strolled across the room to join them.

'Oh, good morning Frobisher. Nice to see you again. Just been having a word with this little lady of yours.'

'It's nice to see you, sir. From what I heard of your word with Miss Marten I gather that you are trying to deprive me of a very competent assistant.'

'Not at all, my boy. Not at all. Just pointing out the folly of getting too far off the beaten track. Can't afford to do it, Frobisher. Can't afford to do it. Remember that.' Having had his say, the older doctor turned and left without waiting for a word from either of them.

Half fearfully Jane looked up at Duncan. For a moment their eyes met before they burst into simultaneous laughter.

'He's a dear, isn't he?' gasped Jane, when she was able to speak again.

'Yes. He's a grand old chap. I didn't realise that you knew him.'

'Oh, yes. He taught me more than all the other lecturers put together. I didn't mention him to you because I never thought of him apart from my own work.'

They were still laughing together as they emerged into the strong sunlight of the busy street. At Duncan's suggestion they made their way through narrow side streets to a small cobbled square which seemed to bear no resemblance to the modern city only a few streets away. They found a small restaurant with brightly painted tables where they were soon seated under a gaily striped canopy. As they savoured the light fragrance of vermouth as golden as the sunlight itself, Jane was aware of the same colourful gaiety and pulsating enjoyment of life as she had discovered in the street scene earlier in the morning.

Their lighthearted mood persisted throughout the meal, although neither of them cared for the trivial exchange of words that so often passes for conversation. Duncan's order for *frittura mista* meant little to Jane, but she found that the food left nothing to be desired and Duncan, in his present mood, was the perfect companion for such a meal. The main dish was made up of a seemingly infinite variety of fragments of meat and vegetables individually coated in crisp batter, so that the pleasure of each mouthful was enhanced by the charm of the unexpected.

As she became aware of Duncan's eyes constantly watching, her self-consciousness made Jane feel clumsy and ungainly in every movement. If she had but realised it, the slight flush on her pale cheeks and her dainty movements as she dealt with the little fritters brought her many appreciative glances from the passers-by. When they were eventually served with strong black coffee, Duncan leant back into the shadow of the canopy and lit his pipe.

'And how do you feel about Hamilton-Ayres's advice?' he asked. His attention appeared to be concentrated on lighting his pipe and she could not judge the mood of the question from the tone of his voice.

'I'm not at all clear what the advice really was,' she countered evasively.

'Oh, come now. Surely he clearly warned you off contemplating matrimony with someone who, in his opinion, was lacking in professional ambition.'

'Yes. I suppose he was, but that is his theme tune for all his women students. We've all heard it too often to take any notice.'

'You can't dismiss H.A. as easily as

that, you know. There is usually pretty good reasoning behind his predictions of death and disaster.'

Jane could find nothing to answer in this, so she maintained silence and wondered to what end the conversation was leading.

'Are you contemplating matrimony, Jane, or was the conversation purely academic?'

The question was, to say the least, unexpected.

'No. Not at present. I mean . . . Yes, it was academic.' Jane was confused by his double question, but she was proud of the casual tone that she summoned up to reply, while her heart cried out to him not to torture her; not to spoil her lovely day.

'Thank goodness for that.' There was an unmistakable note of relief in his voice which immediately caught her attention.

Had she been so transparent then? Had he been afraid that she would create an embarrasing situation by her presence at the clinic? Apparently Duncan considered the subject closed because his next remark was on a point that had arisen during the discussion at the morning meeting of the conference. As they made their way back through the narrow streets his whole attention was apparently absorbed by subjects that had been discussed in the conference room. Jane found herself talking freely again whenever her own field of work was mentioned. The difficult moment at the restaurant was forgotten in a sense of companionship as they talked about how the various points applied to particular children at the clinic.

'I was particularly interested,' she said, 'in what Dr Hamilton-Ayres was saying about the effect of shock on very young children. I wish he could come to the clinic and see David Ives. Do you think it could be arranged?'

At the mention of the child's name Duncan's face hardened into the familiar expressionless mould.

'He saw the child in London,' he said dismissively.

Apparently she had trespassed in suggesting that the visiting specialist could help this child. The strained silence seemed to express more eloquently than words Duncan Frobisher's disapproval of her suggestion. It was as if a door had been opened for a few brief minutes only to be slammed in her face. The pleasant mood of their companionship at the restaurant was lost and, for Jane, the sun seemed to have set on the pleasure of her day. They walked on in silence. Duncan was apparently absorbed again in his own thoughts, which did not include her.

Jane wished fervently that she knew more about David Ives' history. That there was some mystery involved she was quite sure. She had access to all the details of the family background of the other children in her care, but there was no record for David Ives before the account of the injuries caused by the car crash which had killed his mother.

Jane resolved to question Mac about David's family at the earliest opportunity. She felt sure that the key to the child's condition lay somewhere in the story of that crash. For all her care and attention it appeared that David had completely lost his power of speech. He had not uttered an intelligible word since the accident.

The subject of discussion during the afternoon meeting was not of particular interest to Jane and it was only with an effort of willpower that she could keep her attention on what the speakers were saying. At one point her wandering attention came to rest on the handsome features of her companion. Duncan was bending forward in his seat, his whole attention concentrated on the speaker. His expression changed continually as he alternately agreed and disagreed with the opinions stated by the visiting specialist, who was talking about bone injuries in the very young.

From her very first meeting with this strange brother of Max, Jane had been aware of his near dedicated attitude to his work. It was not until now though that she began to feel some of his enthusiasm in herself. Until this day she had thought of little other than the import of her own work in the lives of the children she taught. The mending of their bodily injuries had seemed to her to be some purely mechanical process which would inevitably end in success. Only now, as she listened to the words of the speaker and watched the changing expressions on Duncan's face, did she realise how small a part of the whole scheme was her own.

Once the afternoon meeting was over, Duncan seemed anxious to leave the city at the first opportunity. Jane would have preferred to spend the long light evening exploring the streets and squares, or sitting at one of the many little iron tables on the pavements just watching the passing crowds. On the other hand she was glad to avoid the strain of an intimate evening with this man who was coming to mean more to her with every passing day. As the car sped northward in the rose-tinted sunlight, her thoughts turned to Teresa Ronelli. She wondered if Duncan would be so silent and preoccupied if Teresa were seated beside him, or if he would have been so anxious to return to the clinic. She wondered too how much longer she would be expected to remain at the Villa Alto. Already two of the children under her care had returned to their homes, and two more were due to leave at the end of the month. That would leave her with only two children in her care and surely the clinic could not afford to support her for the sake of only two children.

So immersed was Jane in her own thoughts that she did not notice the slackening speed of the car until they pulled up in front of a village wine shop.

'Just excuse me for one minute.' Duncan was out of the car and had disappeared through the beaded curtain of the doorway before she could

95

question his action. He returned in a matter of moments to help her out of the car.

'I wanted to make sure that they could manage a meal for us before I took you in,' he explained, ushering her into the shop that smelt strongly of garlic mixed with the acrid odours of tobacco smoke and spilled wine. 'We go straight through to the back.'

They passed down a narrow, dark passageway which emerged into a small paved courtyard where three rickety tables were set under a single mulberry tree. There was nobody else in sight as he led her to one of the tables.

'I often eat here when I am alone,' he told her. 'But they don't really cater for passing motorists. I wanted to make sure of some food before I raised your hopes.'

Jane looked round the tiny yard with its few scratching hens and odd assortment of utensils hanging on the house walls. She found it hard to reconcile this humble place with the polished exterior of Duncan Frobisher.

'This is certainly unexpected,' she said. 'Do you know these people then?'

'Yes. I've known them for some time. Young Paolo, their son, was a patient of ours when I first came to Italy and I can always be sure of a friendly welcome here when the world outside seems hard and unkind.'

'Does the world seem hard and unkind today?' she enquired, with a diffident smile.

'On the contrary. The world seems so friendly and kind that I am prepared to take the unprecedented step of sharing my retreat with a specially selected friend.'

His smile was happy and relaxed as he fitted his long form into the small iron chair.

The whole family seemed anxious to join in the serving of the simple meal. It was obvious that Duncan was no casual visitor to them; in every way possible they showed that they looked on him as a loved and respected friend. This was an aspect of him which Jane had not suspected and she found it intriguing. Amid much laughter and talk, which she could only partly share, they were served with plates piled high with saffron gold rissotto followed by a huge bowl of fresh fruit and a local cheese. Jane was not particularly anxious to taste the strong smelling cheese that filled the whole courtyard with its odour. As she sat holding a halting conversation with little Paolo who had singled her out for special attention, Duncan's hand covered hers for a brief moment.

'Take just a little of the cheese to please them,' he murmured. 'It goes well with the wine.'

To her surprise Jane found that the strong flavour of the cheese did indeed blend extremely well with that of the red wine which Duncan had poured into her glass.

It was almost dark before they were once more on their way. As she sat beside him in the car, Jane still felt the touch of his hand on her own. She had a new awareness of him that she could not fight. The need to talk and avoid her own thoughts was too great to allow her to match his silence.

'Thank you for letting me share your retreat. Your friends are such happy people, aren't they?'

'They are a lesson to us all,' he replied gently. 'The art of finding simple happiness is too much neglected. I am glad that you enjoyed their company. It was difficult to decide whether you would prefer to meet Paolo's family or dine to the accompaniment of soft lights and sugary music in a Milan restaurant.'

So he had considered the possibility of spending the evening in Milan after all! That he had decided instead to take her to a village wine shop filled Jane with happiness. A silence settled between them as they neared the end of the journey, but it was the friendly silence of contented companionship. For Jane it was charged with an almost delirious happiness from the knowledge that he had chosen to share his own pleasures with her, rather than to entertain her in the formal artificiality of an expensive restaurant.

When they reached the lakeside town at the foot of the mountain, Duncan did not swing the car into the steeply rising mountain road that led to the clinic, but instead continued to drive round the lakeside. Jane was not left to wonder about this action for long.

'To finish the pleasures of the day we'll spend a short while watching the idle rich enjoying their idleness,' he announced. 'I won't leave you thinking that I don't know how to entertain a feminine companion. You will now take wine amid mink and diamonds and you may fancy yourself a princess — if I may be your prince.'

'To please Your Highness is my own greatest pleasure.' Her tone was gay and her face wore a smile. Only her heart cried out the deep truth of her words as it pounded until it threatened to suffocate her.

The car swung off the road and into a gravelled driveway. The man at the gate saluted Duncan with a friendly greeting in English. They drew up beside a magnificent villa glowing with light from every window. The sound of music drifted towards them as they left the car and walked onto a white-stoned terrace overlooking the lake.

Duncan indicated the lighted windows with a sweeping gesture.

'Here you will find all the international luxury that a big hotel can lavish on its patrons. Here English visitors can eat bacon and eggs for breakfast and Americans can be confident of getting their iced beer. They go home after a stay of a few days and tell their less fortunate friends all about Italy.'

They laughed happily together; Jane found it very easy to laugh that evening.

'You, Jane,' he continued, 'will know a little of the true Italy when the time comes for you to tell your family what you have seen.'

He moved along the terrace to where

white tables were scattered at discreet intervals between decorated pillars. A hovering waiter was immediately beside them, greeting Duncan as though he knew him well.

'Shall we have our drinks here, Jane, or would you rather be indoors?'

Jane's fragile balloon of happiness was rising again to dizzy heights.

'If you don't mind I'd rather stay out here where we can watch the water.'

He nodded agreement and asked the waiter to bring their drinks to the terrace.

'I thought you might like to go inside and watch the fashionable crowd.' His voice held a teasing note. 'Or have I done the unforgivable and brought you here when you don't feel suitably dressed?'

Jane had considered that her neat linen suit was quite suitable for the daytime in Milan but now as she caught glimpses of the silk-clad and bejewelled women through the long uncurtained windows, she realised that she had a good excuse for remaining on the terrace. She seized upon this gratefully.

'I do feel that the competition might be a little unfair,' she answered lightly.

They sat for a while observing the groups of other people who, like themselves, had chosen to enjoy the evening air rather than the bright lights of the hotel rooms. After they had sat for some time in companionable silence, Duncan rose.

'Bring your glass over here,' he said. His hand on her arm led her to the edge of the terrace where a stone balustrade was all that was between them and the dark water of the lake below. The warm evening air was full of subtle scents that were lost in the heat of the day. A water taxi hummed across the lake, leaving a frothy wake that glowed in the silver moonlight. From the hotel behind them floated the sound of an orchestra, occasional bursts of conversation and laughter amid the tinkling of glasses. For Jane there was magic in the air. She was half afraid to speak or even move in case she broke the spell.

'Can you see the Villa Alto?' he asked.

'No. Where?' She looked up at the mountains opposite but she was not sure of the position of the clinic.

He stepped behind her and his arm across her shoulder pointed over the lake to a cluster of lights high up on the other side.

'You see the village?' His voice was close to her ear and she could feel the warmth of his breath on her cheek.

'Now, just to the left. Do you see one small patch of light shining alone?' Jane could not trust her voice to answer. Before she realised it his other arm was encircling her waist, holding her closely in front of him. The voice above her ear held a new quality but the words were conventional enough.

'Now look along my finger. Do you see now?'

Still less able to trust her voice, she nodded. His hands came to rest beside her own on the balustrade so that she stood prisoner in his encircling arms. She could not move until he did. She knew that he had bent his head closer to her own. As she felt his cheek brush her hair she shivered uncontrollably. His lips moved against her hair as he spoke.

'You're cold?' he asked softly.

As she shook her head she felt the momentary touch of his lips on her cheek.

As if from a great distance behind them a woman's voice exclaimed.

'Why, if it isn't Duncan himself.'

The encircling arms stiffened to the accompaniment of a muttered 'Damnation', they dropped to his sides as Duncan Frobisher turned to meet the newcomers.

The woman who was crossing the terrace towards them was in formal evening dress as was the man who accompanied her. Behind them walked Max Frobisher and Teresa Ronelli.

Duncan performed the introductions

between Jane and the new couple who proved to be Americans. Jane never heard their name as she struggled to regain enough composure to join in the chatter of the foursome who were obviously in a lighthearted, after-dinner mood.

During the conversation it was mentioned that the other couple had collected Teresa and Max earlier in the evening so it was inevitable that the four from the Villa Alto should return there in Duncan's car. Duncan terminated the evening's entertainment as quickly as courtesy would allow.

'I am sorry that we must go,' he said pleasantly, 'but I have already kept Miss Marten out too long without a coat. She was shivering so much that we had just decided to go when you came out.' This was spoken without a glance at Jane who was grateful to escape from the terrace and all its associations as quickly as possible.

They covered the short distance to the clinic at an alarming speed. Duncan with Teresa beside him drove with a furious concentration that bore no relationship to his handling of the car earlier in the day. Jane, in the back beside Max, found none of her usual pleasure in the company of Duncan's brother.

When at last she was alone in her room she tried to think calmly of those moments on the hotel terrace before they had been interrupted. Carefully she recalled every word that had been spoken and equally carefully she interpreted them in the only way that seemed to make sense. Nothing had happened except that Duncan had emphasized his pointing out of the clinic by turning her in the right direction. If she had not shaken her head she would never have felt that fleeting touch of his lips. That was all that could have happened. It must be all.

Jane's thoughts turned unhappily to the arrival of Teresa Ronelli. She could remember nothing in Duncan's attitude that showed special attention to Teresa except that she had driven back beside him.

One thing was quite certain. She now knew beyond any doubt that it was Duncan Frobisher whom she loved, and loved so greatly that she could not stay much longer at the clinic — to be near him every day would be to be in constant fear of betraying herself.

The morning that followed the Milan visit was as bright and clear as she had come to expect Italian mornings to be. The sunshine and the cloudless sky helped to dispel the depression that had settled over Jane's unhappy thoughts during a wakeful night. Resolved not to think about her own problems, she turned to her work with that almost feverish energy which owes its existence to the dread of having time to think. She sought out Mary Mackinlay and bluntly asked what the older woman knew about David Ives. Mac was evasive. While admitting that there possibly was more to tell than Jane knew, she suggested that Duncan was the person who should give her the information.

Determined to cure her present depression by the most radical treatment, Jane sought an interview with Duncan that very afternoon. It was not until she was told that he would see her immediately that she realised how foolishly unprepared for the encounter she was. As she crossed his secretary's room to enter the library by the communicating door, her legs suddenly ceased to feel real; how she crossed the library to Duncan's desk she never could remember.

'You wanted to see me, Jane?' His manner was friendly as he put aside the report that he was reading and prepared to give her his full attention.

Gratefully she sank into the chair that was provided for just such interviews.

'Yes. I want to discuss the case of one of my pupils.' Jane never referred to her charges as patients as all the other members of the clinic staff did.

'Oh. Which one is that?' enquired Duncan, as he turned to the cabinet which contained the case-files of the children currently at the clinic.

'David Ives,' she announced firmly.

There was a sudden stiffening of Duncan's body as he paused in the act of opening the filing cabinet. The pause was only momentary, but Jane was watching for his reaction. Inexplicable though it was, that hesitation did not pass unnoticed and she determined to get to the bottom of this mystery. She watched him select the file and place it on his desk.

'David doesn't present the same problem as my other pupils,' she stated, carefully keeping her eyes on his expressionless face. 'I don't seem to be having any success with him and I need your help.'

'How can I help you with young David?' His voice was normal but there was an underlying note of caution in his tone and Jane detected it instantly.

'By telling me the background to his

case,' she stated positively.

Again the slight stiffening of his body as he glanced across the desk —

'Surely you have read the file?' he queried. His voice was no longer warm and personal. The enigmatic, aloof medical superintendent of the Villa Alto clinic faced her as she had seen him at their first meeting.

'I have read the file a number of times,' she replied calmly, 'but it gives me no clue to work on. The child's problem is outside my normal field, but I am sure that I could help him if I only knew more about his circumstances.'

There was a heavy silence before Duncan spoke.

'I am afraid that I can't help you there, Jane. This file is your guide to the case and I can't tell you any more.' There was a note of finality in his words, but Jane was not to be deflected from her purpose.

'You can,' she stated, with a resolution which surprised herself, 'and if you have the child's welfare at heart you will. I know that I could help if only . . . ' Her speech trailed off as she regarded Duncan in suddenly wide-eyed amazement.

As she was speaking she was pleading on behalf of the dear speechless little boy whose welfare was so much her concern. Her voice failed suddenly as a vivid picture of the child presented itself to her mind's eye. Sudden revelation turned suspicion into certainty as she stared at Duncan — the two were related; the tall dark man and the cherubic, curly-haired child in the nursery. If she could have recalled the words that she had just spoken, Jane would willingly have done so in that moment.

Duncan sat motionless. His usually inscrutable countenance showed that he was making a difficult decision. His gaze rested reflectively on Jane's troubled face. When he spoke his voice was quiet but resolute.

'All right, Jane. I certainly owe it to you by now. His full name is David Ives Frobisher. He is my son.'

There was an astounded silence in

the room during which Jane wished that the marble floor could open and swallow her down. It seemed a long time before she could find her voice.

'I'm . . . I'm so sorry. I didn't know.'

'Of course you didn't.' He answered in a quietly gentle tone, as he turned from her to gaze thoughtfully out of the long window behind his desk.

Watching him now she was amazed that she had not recognised the likeness before. Undoubtedly it was this likeness that had found David his special place in her heart from the very first. When Duncan spoke again, his speech was clipped in a manner which signified a depth of emotion of which she would not have believed him capable.

'I should be grateful if you would not mention this among the staff. I've never used David's full name here on purpose to avoid idle talk. Only Mrs Mackinlay knows the whole story.'

Jane's tender heart was touched by the tragic situation. The thought of the dear speechless little boy in the nursery brought a wave of sympathy for the three people whose lives had been so disastrously affected by a car crash. She wondered how to end this conversation on a subject that was perhaps still too painful to discuss and obviously no concern of hers. She rose from her chair with a gesture to indicate that she was prepared to accept what he had told her without further explanation.

'Of course I will keep your confidence. I can only say how — how sorry I am that I didn't respect your wishes in the first place. If I could take back my part in this conversation, believe me, I would.' She turned to the doorway and then paused. 'I can only promise to do my best to forget it,' she added quietly, and then thought what a pointless remark that was. As if she was ever likely to forget this conversation!

As she turned again to the door, he was still standing gazing out of the window, but her words recalled his attention and he glanced across the room at her with suddenly sharpened interest.

Although Jane was not to know his thoughts, she was conscious of his scrutiny. His main feeling was one of surprise — surprise that her womanly curiosity had not prompted her to ask why he kept his son close to him and yet tacitly denied his identity — a question which he could hardly answer to himself. His usual calm gave way.

'Jane — Miss Marten. Oh, hell! Wait a minute.' The staccato utterances were so unlike the usual measured speech of the habitually self-contained Duncan that Jane recrossed the room towards him at once. Instinctively she was returning at the call of the man rather than on the order of her employer; she did not return to the chair that was placed to face the desk but went to stand beside him. Her hand rested on the desk beside his.

'I really am sorry,' she said simply. He smiled wryly down at her as his hand moved to cover her own. There was a reflective look in his grey eyes.

'And what are you so sorry about?

You were only doing your job to the best of your ability.' His voice was serious but there was a quizzical smile lurking about his eyes.

'For making you talk when you would have preferred not to,' she replied.

He smiled at her again and patted the hand beneath his with an oddly diffident gesture.

'Sit down, Jane. I want to tell you a bit more.'

'Please, there is no need.' She knew that she was blushing uncontrollably. 'If I had known that it concerned you so personally I would not have been so outrageously curious.'

With one of his lightening changes of mood he laughed almost gaily.

'So now you tell me that it was curiosity that prompted your questions and not professional zeal. Forgive me for teasing you, Jane, you would not be a natural woman if you had not been curious in the face of my evasions. And you would certainly not be a woman if you were not more curious now.'

His smile took away any possible sting from his words as he seated himself opposite her once more.

'It's not a very pleasant story, even in outline.' His tone was hard.

'You sound very bitter.' She was amazed at her own temerity in venturing such a remark.

'Bitter? Yes, I suppose I am.' He sat, apparently considering this aspect of himself.

'The accident must have been a terrible shock to you,' she said gently. 'Your wife's death, I mean.'

'I had not seen my wife for some years when it happened. The shock was more for the child.' His voice was hard and bitter again.

'Poor David,' said Jane softly. 'He must miss his mother terribly.' She realised that the subject was delicate; that she must choose her words carefully. The more so because her own heart clamoured to offer sympathy to the two survivors of the unhappy trio.

'David never knew his mother.' The statement left a stark silence to fill the lofty, book-lined room while the sun streamed across the terrace beyond the windows. When Duncan spoke again it was in the same carefully clipped tones that he had used earlier when referring to David.

'We were divorced and I had custody of the child. He was with my sister — you know Celia and Edward Gresham, I believe. His mother arrived out of the blue one day and drove off with the child before anyone knew what had happened. What prompted her to do it nobody knows.' He paused for a moment. 'The crash happened half an hour later,' he added with a note of finality.

Jane had listened attentively without attempting to interrupt. Now she bit her lip to control its betrayal of her emotion.

'Oh,' she said inadequately; and then, feeling that some further comment was called for, she continued, almost unconsciously thinking aloud. 'I know that there are always many sides to these problems — but it must be terrible for any mother to be forced to part with her child.'

'There was no forcing of the parting. She left the child and myself when David was barely three months old.'

'How could she?' Jane's voice was scarcely more than a whisper.

'She had compensations, in the plural,' Duncan assured her grimly. 'She was a charming, elegant woman who took exactly what she wanted from life at any particular moment.' His voice was reminiscent but devoid of any nostalgic warmth.

'But she was your wife,' thought Jane, noticing the lines of strain that radiated from those remote grey eyes. As if divining her thoughts, his eyes met hers with a tired smile.

'It's not a very nice story, is it? But we can all make mistakes, Jane.' He spoke slowly and carefully. 'Even those of us who pride ourselves on our sound judgement. Especially in matters of the heart,' he added.

Jane was confused and searched her mind desperately for some suitable remark. Gratefully her thoughts returned to little David.

'You know that I will do all that I can for David,' she said a trifle breathlessly.

He smiled at her.

'Yes, I know you will. I have felt guilty about keeping up the deception with you from the beginning. Now that the sordid story is told there is a strange relief in knowing that it is shared with you.' He was speaking very quietly and the last two words were almost inaudible. Jane hardly knew whether she had heard them or supplied them from her own imagination.

There seemed no point in prolonging this embarrassing conversation and once again Jane rose to leave. As she stood for a moment, she reflected that it seemed impossible that it was less than an hour since she had entered the library in such a militant mood. Soon all the frustration of her own problems would return with renewed force, but for this one afternoon at least her own affairs had faded into insignficance. She glanced at her watch and exclaimed in surprise.

'Oh dear, I have a class in five minutes.'

'Yes, we must both go about our business.' Once again his tone was formal. 'We'll talk about David's future another time.'

It was a dismissal that held a promise of the continuation of their new, confidential relationship. As she crossed to the door, he was beside her and once again their hands met as they closed on the door handle together.

'Did I tell you that you are a very nice person, Jane?' he asked conversationally. So unexpected were the words that he surprised a blush as she looked up at him. 'I was about to tell you so when our last conversation was so unfortunately interrupted.'

The ringing of the telephone on the desk shrilled insistently through the still air of the room. Duncan glanced at the instrument with apparent distaste. His hand closed more closely over hers as he pressed on the heavy door handle.

'Thank you,' she murmured, inadequately.

'No, Jane. I thank you. Thank you a thousand times for being yourself.'

The door was open and the telephone still shrilled boisterously. In a daze she stepped into the hallway and turned to meet his eyes once more before the heavy door closed between them.

It was several hours before Jane was free to seek the sanctuary of her own room. At last she could close the door and allow the emotional tide of the day to flood over her. Numbly she crossed the room to the little balcony and gazed unseeingly across the horizon of alpine peaks. The view that had always thrilled her awoke no enthusiasm tonight. She had no emotion to spare for the inanimate mountains. Slowly her gaze lowered to the terrace below until it focused on a moving patch of white. It was the petite figure of Teresa Ronelli making her way across the shadowy terrace towards the library windows.

In a struggle of painful self-examination, Jane faced the insoluble problem presented by the undeniable fact that she loved Duncan Frobisher. She loved him as she had never known love before and in the library below at this moment he must be greeting Teresa with all the love that he would offer to his intended bride.

* * *

The whole senior staff of the clinic had apparently been invited to the party for Teresa Ronelli, but it was obvious that two people at least would have to remain on night duty. Hoping that this might save her from a nerve-racking ordeal, Jane approached Matron with an offer to remain on duty for the night. As she was only temporarily employed at the clinic, she explained, she felt that it was more fitting that the permanent staff should go. Matron was graciously pleased with her offer but firmly declined it. Her nurses, she assured Jane, expected to make these little sacrifices in the course of their duty. Resigning herself to the dictates of authority, Jane dismissed the idea of developing a convenient headache. To the party she must go.

The evening of the great event brought a flurry of preparation as dresses were finally donned and the air of the clinic was filled with the unusual fragrance of feminine perfumes.

The girls were to be driven the short distance to the Ronelli home in the doctors' cars. Jane stood in her room and prayed fervently that she could arrange to drive with Mario or Max rather than Duncan. A spray of exotic Italian blossoms had arrived with a gay little card inscribed by Mario wishing her a happy evening. With a wry smile Jane detached the card with its almost mocking message and held the spray against her shoulder of her simple dress; the same pale green dress that had so impressed Max on her last evening in England. When the flowers were firmly pinned in place, Jane made her way down the staircase, determined to show the world a face of gaiety and laughter to match the blossoms that belonged to the sunlight of Italy.

It appeared that Duncan was still occupied by work and Max was gaily running a ferry service for what he described as the 'bevy of beauty'. Jane had never known him to be more gallantly debonair than he was as they drove to the party.

'You seem very happy tonight, Max,' Jane laughed, as he beat a tattoo on the horn.

'I am the happiest man in the world, and I want you all to know it,' he assured everyone within hearing, with an extravagant pseudo-American accent that left the whole carload helpless with laughter.

'And that reminds me, Jane,' he continued, when the mirth had subsided, 'What about our date with Milan? You can't let all work make Jane a dull girl.'

5

The question obviously required no particular answer so that Jane was able to retort 'Dull yourself!' and therewith dismiss the subject. Further banter was cut short by their arrival in front of the long, low villa in which the Ronelli family now made their home.

It was Jane's first visit and she looked around with great interest at the rich simplicity that typified every visible possession of the household. Here was wealth displayed where it gave pleasure to its owner and his guests alike without a trace of vulgarity or ostentation.

The party was already well under way when they arrived. Max introduced Jane to some English-speaking friends of Teresa's and shepherded the rest of his party onward. It was not long before a young Italian claimed Jane for her first dance of the evening and led her onto the floor.

After the dance it was with difficulty that Jane persuaded the young man to leave her to her own devices. He was reluctant to leave her without a partner, but eventually he left her when she convinced him that she wanted to talk with Dorothy Archer. Jane had very little contact with the red-headed nurse from the Villa Alto during their working days, but now she found the girl grateful for her company and together they enjoyed the spectacle of the other guests dancing or standing in conversational groups about the magnificent room. Jane doubted whether Christine Powell would have tolerated the role of interested onlooker for long. It was Matron's decree that Dorothy should attend the party and Christine remain on duty. The arrangement did not suit either of the English girls particularly well, but the authority of the decision was unquestionable. Jane learned this story from Dorothy and was grateful to

Matron for unwittingly providing her with a partner.

Mario paused by Jane and Dorothy for a moment to remind both girls to save him a dance in the later part of the evening when his duties as son of the house would take less of his attention. Seeing that the two girls were without partners, he reappeared a few minutes later to introduce two unknown young men who ceremoniously led the girls onto the dance floor. Jane was highly amused by the courtly formality of the procedure and once again found great difficulty in detaching her partner when they returned to find Dorothy still missing. The young man was only persuaded to abandon her by the fact that he was already engaged for the next dance.

The room was very full of chattering, laughing guests; the air was heady with the scent of the women's perfumes and the many flowers that decorated the walls. Jane found herself a cool spot by one of the long windows that stood open onto the terrace. Very soon she was grateful for this position as she saw Signore Ronelli rise and call the attention of the guests around him. Gradually a hush fell over the entire company. This was the moment she had dreaded for so long. Grateful for the opportunity, Jane slipped through the open window to the terrace that was softly lit by the light of a brilliantly full moon above and the lights of the room behind her. Here she could say a lonely goodbye to her impossible dreams.

As she stood alone in the warm night, Jane realised that a wild hope had been hovering in her mind ever since the night on which Mario had told her of the forthcoming engagement: the hope that two years of a full musical career would have altered Teresa's attitude to marriage. She might have known that with Duncan such a thing would be impossible. He had loved and lost heavily once and he was not a man to gamble for such stakes twice. When Duncan chose his second wife it would be a careful, quietly happy decision that would admit no second thoughts.

A movement of someone standing by the bushes that bordered the terrace caused her to start guiltily. Who else was playing truant from the crowded party to disturb her private moment of pain?

'Running away?' queried a sardonic voice from the shadows. Duncan Frobisher strolled forward into the light of the open terrace. His smile was mocking and somehow a cruel reminder of their first encounter.

As he strolled purposefully towards her, Jane stood speechless. Why, oh why, would he not leave her alone? Already they must be looking for him inside. 'Please, please,' she pleaded silently, 'just go back to her and leave me alone.'

'Sad maid in the moonlight, you have a lesson to learn.' His voice still held the half mocking tone of their earlier meetings.

Unhappily Jane stood rigidly upright, not daring to look at him, but gazing down to the lighted valley and the glistening lake far below. In a flash of painfully vivid recollection she relived the other occasion when they had stood side by side on a terrace overlooking the lake.

'A lesson?' she queried dully.

'This lesson.' His voice was as hard and pitiless as the lips that met hers in a demanding kiss that was almost savage in its lack of gentleness. A kiss that drew all the resistance from her body. Nor did he release her easily. His lips that a moment before had crushed her own with such painful intensity hovered tantalisingly, compelling an answering yielding to their silent call before he turned abruptly to the lighted windows.

'Come and toast the happy pair.' There was no escaping the grip that propelled her into the chattering throng that filled the brightly lit room.

Still conscious of little other than Duncan's burning grip on her arm, Jane halted as her eyes followed the direction of the gaze of the assembled guests. On the platform that held the small orchestra stood Signore Ronelli clasping the joined hands of two people whose happy smiles proclaimed their love for all to see. Teresa had never looked more lovely than on this night and the debonair charm of Max Frobisher was her perfect complement.

Jane stared mutely until comprehension brought overwhelming relief.

'It's Max,' she murmured, 'Max . . . '

The floor moved slowly from beneath her feet; the room became unbearably hot and strangely dark.

The cool air of the terrace caressed her face kindly as she drew unsteadily away from Duncan's supporting arm.

'All right now?' His voice was curiously soft and kind. 'I'll see you home.'

'No, no, I'm all right now,' she protested weakly. 'It was only the heat.'

Ignoring her protest, he led her firmly round the house to his waiting car and half-lifted her into the passenger seat. They drove the short distance between the villas in silence.

The sight of the familiar entrance roused Jane from her dazed state, but before she could react to their arrival, a strong arm was guiding her through the doorway. The old villa was steeped in heavy silence. They crossed the great hallway, their footsteps echoing hollowly on the marble floor.

At the foot of the staircase Duncan paused as if to speak; the guiding hand on her arm tightened its grip, but the words that might have been spoken were never uttered because the sound of a childish treble suddenly broke the enveloping silence.

'Daddy. My Daddy,' it wailed.

The voice came from the gallery above them. It was quickly followed by the sound of running feet and Christine Powell's unmistakable voice called 'Come back here.' But the pattering feet continued and through the open balustrade the silent watchers at the foot of the staircase saw a small pyjama-clad figure making its purposeful way across the wide gallery.

The grip on Jane's arm tightened convulsively for a second and then Duncan's long legs were carrying him up the staircase at a pace that bore no relationship to the normally unhurried progress of the medical superintendent of the Villa Alto.

As Jane began to follow Duncan up the staircase, Matron's voice was heard coming from the direction of the nurseries. 'What is the trouble, nurse?' The sharp tone indicated that there would indeed be trouble for someone unless there was a satisfactory explanation for the present disturbance.

Christine's footsteps had stopped momentarily. 'It is David Ives, Matron. He is out of bed and calling for his father.' Matron and nurse emerged together from the nursery corridor that led onto the gallery.

'It's all right, Matron,' Duncan's voice was quiet but very firm. 'The young man is safe and sound.' The three women stood motionless watching the two dark heads that were so close together.

Duncan was seated on the top step of the stairs and the troubled little boy had hurled himself into the man's outstretched arms with a single long-drawn sob.

Christine Powell stepped forward quietly and took the whimpering child gently by the shoulders. 'Come back to bed now David,' she said in a soft voice that contrasted oddly with her usual crisp tones.

David turned momentarily in instinctive obedience, but after one glance at the tall fair nurse he shook himself free and with a sharp cry of 'My Daddy!' he threw his little body at Duncan again.

Duncan's arms enclosed the sobbing child. 'All right, little man,' he murmured. 'It's all right now. Quietly does it.' His head was bent so that his face was hidden against the child's trembling body.

The sight of the two dark heads together, the man's smooth and shining and the child's curly and tumbled, brought an almost physical pain to

Jane's heart as she stood above them. She loved them both with all the depth and tenderness of a woman's love and she could no longer deny it to herself. She knew that it was for her to rescue Duncan from this predicament.

The skirts of her long dress rustled as she knelt beside the two on the staircase. David glanced up at the sound and favoured her with a watery smile.

'David,' she said quietly. 'Will you come back to bed with me now?' The child hesitated as he glanced up at the waiting nurses and then back to Duncan. His lips began to tremble again.

'My Daddy,' he insisted tremulously.

'Yes, darling,' Jane's voice was gentle and low. 'I know that you want your Daddy, but daddies have to go to sleep too, you see. It is time for all little boys and their daddies to sleep now. Everybody's Daddy is asleep.' As she was speaking she took the unresisting child into her arms with great care not to interrupt his view of Duncan during the transfer. Her voice continued, gently caressing the worried little boy. 'Will you come with me now and go to sleep like your Daddy does?'

The soft tones had lulled the tired child so that he was resting his little head against her shoulder and a cherubic smile was her only answer as heavy lids fluttered over sleepy eyes. With a last sleepy glance at Duncan and a murmured 'Daddy' he snuggled more closely into her arms and, childlike, was asleep. Jane had not dared to look at Duncan Frobisher in all this time. Now their eyes met briefly. She could not read his expression but an almost imperceptible nod indicated that she was in charge of the situation before he stretched his long form and helped her to her feet with the sleeping child.

The two nurses, who had stood silently by sensing an unusual situation, stepped aside to let Jane pass. As she took her first step forward her toe caught in the hem of her long dress and for a moment her balance was precarious. She turned to the waiting nurse.

'Nurse Powell, have you a safety pin?' she asked. The question broke the tense atmosphere and an air of normality returned to the little group at the head of the staircase.

While Christine Powell pinned up Jane's long skirt, Duncan spoke quietly with Matron and then crossed to Jane's side.

'Would you join us in Matron's office when he is safely in bed?' he asked quietly. There was all the old peremptory command in the quietly spoken request, but Jane thought that she could detect a more personal note below the surface. With a silent nod of assent she left them.

When the unconscious cause of the disturbance had unprotestingly snuggled down into his bed once more, Jane left him in the care of the Italian night nurse and made her way to Matron's office. As the heels of her evening shoes clicked sharply across the marbled floor of the gallery once more, Jane wondered how much longer this seemingly endless night would last. If she could have avoided meeting Duncan Frobisher again she would have turned and fled, at that moment, but she had agreed to return and she knew that she must.

With a gentle tap on the door, she turned the handle and entered the brightly lit room. Matron's cheerful small room which served as her office and sitting room had a cosy atmosphere that was a welcome antidote to the emotional tension of the day.

'Come and sit down, Miss Marten.' Duncan's solicitous tone almost broke the careful façade that hid her unhappiness.

They had obviously been discussing the later events of the evening when she arrived. Apparently David had been unusually restless for most of the day; ever since the father of a departing child had arrived to collect his jubilant offspring. The little girl had seen her father's taxi arrive and had dashed about the playroom telling all and sundry — 'It's my Daddy . . . My Daddy has come . . . I've seen my Daddy.'

Jane's tired brain could hardly take in what they were saying, but suddenly she sat forward with a silent exclamation on her lips. As quickly she sank back again, reflecting that this was not her province, but the movement had not been lost on Duncan.

'Yes, Jane. Go on,' he said. 'What were you going to say?'

'Well, it's not really my field,' she replied diffidently, 'but I would like to ask Matron a question.'

'Go on then.' He was watching her intently.

'What is it, Miss Marten?' enquired Matron, her kindly tone tinged with a hint of suspicion, as it always was if anyone appeared to be trespassing on her jealously guarded preserves.

'I was only going to ask if it isn't more usual for the mothers to collect the children when they leave.'

The expressions of the two nurses indicated that they considered this an irrelevant remark, but Matron smiled indulgently.

'Yes, Miss Marten. I think it is more usual,' she replied, in a tone that indicated that Jane had now been allowed her say and perhaps she would leave the 'professionals' to continue their work. But Duncan was not so ready to dismiss Jane's contribution. He leant forward eagerly as though what she was saying intrigued him.

'Go on, Jane.' He spoke quietly.

'Well . . . ' she glanced round the three faces and decided that it would be diplomatic to address her remarks to Matron. 'It seems strange that David should speak so suddenly and clearly after so long. He must have been very excited about something.' Encouraged by their attention she continued by asking a question. 'Is it possible that this is the first time that David has known a father to call for a child, rather than a mother?'

They looked to Matron who nodded. 'Quite possible.'

Jane bit her lip reflectively. 'I wonder,' she said, 'if that was what roused his memory.' Carefully fixing her gaze on the patterned carpet she continued. 'Dr Frobisher has told me that David hardly knew his mother but that he spent a considerable time with his father before the accident.' She paused and then spoke slowly and carefully. 'If he had developed a very strong affection for a father whom he associated with long absences and joyful reunions, then today's events might have touched just the spring of memory that was needed.'

Christine Powell was the first to speak. 'Do you think that he will go on talking now?' she asked eagerly; her usual languid pose forgotten in the enthusiasm of the moment.

Jane smiled ruefully and shook her head. She dared not glance at Duncan.

'There I am not qualified to give an opinion.' Everybody seemed to be waiting for her to say more. 'I can only say I hope so. Oh, I hope so.' To her consternation the last words came out in an uncontrollable sob and her hands flew to cover her face.

Duncan's cool voice sounded firmly

through the uncomfortable silence. 'Goodnight Matron, Nurse. I'll see you again first thing in the morning.' A hand below Jane's elbow supported her as she rose from her chair, pale but once again in control of herself.

On the gallery once more, Duncan paused and turned to speak to Jane, but for the second time that night his words were cut short by the sound of footsteps. A man's heavy footfall sounded on the stairs and Max bounded into view.

'Oh, there you are,' he exclaimed. 'We wondered what had happened to you. Are you all right, Jane?'

'Yes, I'm all right, thank you Max.' But Max was not satisfied.

'Somebody said that they had seen Duncan helping you out. Teresa sent me over to see what had happened.'

Duncan's deeper voice cut across his brother's lively tenor. 'Jane got a bit of a headache in the hot room and I brought her home. That's all that was wrong.'

'Well I must say that you both look a bit peaky.' Max peered at them in the dim light of the gallery. 'I say, have you two seen a ghost or something? You look mighty odd to me.'

Duncan laughed quietly. 'Thanks for the compliment. As a matter of fact we have had a bit of a shock.'

'Oh dear!' moaned Max, in mock agony. 'Not tonight! What's gone wrong?'

'Nothing is wrong, Max,' Jane told him, 'but you see . . . ' She glanced at Duncan uncertainly, but he nodded.

'You tell him,' he said.

'Well, just as we got here we were greeted by David. He was demanding his father in very audible tones.'

Max looked from one to the other incredulously. 'You mean that he was really talking?'

Duncan laughed again and the sound had a happy note for the first time in the long evening. 'You couldn't exactly call it good conversation,' he said, 'but it was a loud and emphatic opening gambit.'

Max let out a suppressed whoop of joy. 'Jane, you wonderful, wonderful girl! I love you!' he exclaimed. Before she realised his intention, Jane found herself swept off her feet as a hearty kiss landed resoundingly on her cheek.

Duncan's most icy tones brought Max to a sudden halt in the middle of executing a waltzing turn with Jane still in his arms.

'Max. Stop acting like a young fool. Put Miss Marten down and get back to your celebrations.' Max grinned sheepishly as he restored Jane to her feet.

'Sorry old man,' he said, cheerfully. 'I'm not really pickled you know. It is grand news.'

Duncan's stern expression relaxed into a grudging smile. 'Thank you, Max. Now take yourself off, please. It has been a hectic night and we want some peace and quiet here. You are not a peaceful chap to have around at present, so kindly remove yourself.'

Max grinned irrepressibly at them both. 'Tyrant,' he muttered as he raised his hand in a gay salute before he bounded away down the staircase. Jane could not suppress a small laugh.

'I'm glad that you find something to amuse you,' Duncan remarked. His expression dispelled the light-hearted mood that Max had brought into the quiet clinic.

'It's just that I find it very difficult, at times, to remember that Max is a doctor,' she told him. Duncan looked at her with evident surprise but he made no further comment. His tone when addressing Max had been one of annoyance tempered by almost paternal indulgence. There was no doubt, Jane reflected, that although the brothers were twins Duncan was the elder by common consent.

Although she was weary and emotionally exhausted, Jane felt that she could not refuse Duncan's coolly formal request to join him in the library for a few minutes. As they descended the staircase in silence she recalled the events of the crowded day and shrank from facing Duncan alone. In his present mood who knew what she might have to contend with when the library door closed behind them? Apprehensively she stepped in front of him to enter the familiar room that had witnessed so much of what had passed between them in the short time since their first meeting.

The deliberate silence that persisted while Duncan moved across the room to switch on a lamp before he turned to face her did nothing to increase Jane's confidence. When he spoke the old sardonic smile played across his well-formed features.

'Have a cigarette,' he suggested. 'You deserve it after that excellent performance. I must congratulate you.'

Jane leaned unsteadily forward to take the proffered light for her cigarette while she puzzled over the meaning of his words. When she raised her head, he was regarding her with seemingly unfriendly, mocking eyes.

'I'm afraid I don't understand what you mean.' The lift of her head as she met his gaze was instinctive. It was also oddly reminiscent of their first meeting in that room; an unconsciously defiant little gesture that, to one who knew her, betrayed her lack of confidence more surely than any words could have done. Duncan's smile softened momentarily as his eyes held hers.

'Sit down, Jane,' he said, turning to his accustomed seat behind the great desk. 'If you choose not to understand me, then we'll leave it at that.'

Something in his tone sharpened Jane's attention. She realised that he was pale and strained. Duncan too was obviously feeling the impact of the evening's happenings.

'Now tell me how we can best help young David.' His tone was non-committal but she knew that the problem was vital to him. Dragging her mind back from the puzzling implications of his earlier remarks, she concentrated on his present request.

'I'm afraid that I have no constructive suggestion to make,' she replied thoughtfully. 'We can only wait and see what tomorrow brings.'

'And do you think it will bring any progress, Jane?'

She shook her head sadly. 'I am not in a position to judge.'

'Oh come, Jane.' His tone was impatient but tinged with a gentleness he rarely showed. 'Forget your professional caution for a moment and tell me what you really think. After all, you have plenty of experience on which to base an opinion.'

It was Jane's turn to smile. 'And what would you say if someone asked you to forget your professional caution?' she queried.

Duncan smiled back at her and passed a hand across his eyes. The gesture told her how near he was to her own state of emotional exhaustion.

'Touché,' he murmured, favouring her with a grin that held much of Max's boyish spirit. 'So you are not going to offer me any hope that tonight's change may be lasting.'

'Oh yes!' she exclaimed impulsively. 'I do hope. Most sincerely I do. For both your sakes.' As she spoke the last words her voice dropped to scarcely more than a whisper.

'Thank you, Jane. I know I can't ask for more than that.' They sat smoking in silence for some minutes. He gave an odd, short laugh before he spoke again. 'The tables have really turned on me, haven't they? It is usually I who have to be non-committal and careful not to inspire unreasonable hope in anxious parents.'

Again there was silence between them. Jane could find no words adequate to answer his. There was obviously no more to be said that night. Carefully she stubbed out her cigarette and rose to leave the room, but before she could speak he was beside her.

'Before you go, Jane . . . '

The peace and quiet of the great room had seeped into her mind and restored some of her former balance. Gently Jane placed a hand on his arm and interrupted him.

'Please, Duncan.' In the stress of the moment she was unconscious of the use of his name. 'Whatever you were going to say, will it keep until another time?'

He was very close to her and with awareness of the physical contact of her hand resting on his arm, panic rose again. Whatever happened she must prevent him from referring to the earlier happenings of this eventful night, particularly to the few brief minutes when they were alone on the terrace. She attempted a light laugh as she self-consciously lowered the detaining hand from his arm.

'The traditional stiff upper lip only lasts so long.' She tried to speak flippantly but her voice suddenly broke. 'And . . . and I'm afraid I'm going to cry,' she added with a gasp as she snatched up her long skirt and ran from the room.

It was not imminent tears that caused Jane's hurried exit so much as a sudden realisation that she wanted nothing so much as to rest her head against Duncan's shoulder, to have his strong arms about her and feel again the touch of her lips on her own. The desire was so powerful that she had to escape or succumb and throw herself into his arms.

Once in her own room, Jane stood braced against the door with closed eyes and wondered at the almost over-powering strength of her own emotions. One thing was certain. She could not stay much longer in the place which brought her into daily contact with Duncan Frobisher after that kiss which, so far from expressing any tenderness, had been a painful mockery of her love — as if he wished to punish her for the very act of loving. She could be thankful at least that at present he believed her love to be for Max, but she could not hide behind that tacit lie much longer.

There was a painful dryness in her eyes when she opened them. A sob escaped from her throat and the burning tears could be held back no longer.

★　★　★

The following morning Jane had little time to think of her own affairs as she washed and dressed hurriedly. She had to get to David as soon as possible, before anyone tried to be helpful and encourage him to talk. When she arrived at the nursery she was thankful to find the sensible Dorothy Archer on duty. David was romping happily in some game that involved two chairs and a length of string. The purpose of the game never appeared clearly enough for an adult mind to grasp, but the children were obviously happy in their occupation. After a few moments the game ended and Jane collected her particular charges. She said 'Hallo' to each of them in turn. Some echoed her greeting while the others indicated their acknowledgement, each in the individual manner which they had adopted to overcome their inability to speak.

David was last of the four for her greeting. He moved quietly to her side while she was speaking to the other children and slipped a confiding hand into hers. 'Hallo, David,' she said encouragingly.

The response was an enchanting grin, but no words came.

'Aren't you going to say hallo this morning?' asked Jane, in a tone that indicated that this was the first time that such a lapse had occurred.

The little boy shook his dark head emphatically. It had long ago been established that David heard every word that was spoken to him, and understood most.

Jane had not realised how confident she had been until she experienced the bitter disappointment of the child's lack of response. With forced cheerfulness she shrugged dismissively as she returned the smile of the adorable imp whose hand still held her own.

'Shall we all go to breakfast now?' she asked the assembled company. The idea was greeted with a delighted outburst. Jane did not usually take her meals with the children and the event was obviously regarded as a special treat.

Throughout the morning David was never far from her side, and although he appeared happy enough, Jane was aware that something was troubling the little boy.

When Duncan arrived on his daily round, the children were playing quietly in two pairs. David, close to Jane, was very much occupied with a toy train. The child was too close for discussion so, in response to the query of Duncan's raised eyebrows, Jane could only shake her head in a sad negative. Together they looked down at his son who favoured them both with his most enchanting smile as he sent his engine careering across the floor away from them.

'Never mind, Jane.' Duncan spoke in the precise, clipped tone that she had become accustomed to when he was speaking of his personal affairs. 'At least we know that it is possible. That is certainly a comforting thought. I always knew it in theory, of course, but there is nothing like a practical demonstration to prove the point.' They smiled at each other in mutual understanding.

'There are times when he can be so very human,' Jane thought with a mental shrug as their talk turned to other aspects of her work.

As they stood and talked, a small hand crept into Jane's and pulled to claim her attention. She glanced down to see David gazing up at her, a worried frown creasing his usually smooth brow. 'H . . . Ha . . . Hallo.' It was a small voice but quite distinct with only a slight hesitation over the difficult consonant.

She sensed the stiffening of Duncan's body beside her and another larger, stronger hand found hers in that moment. Fractionally Jane's attention was diverted before her long years of training took control. This was the time that always called for her greatest effort — the instant when one of her pupils uttered the first word, after months, sometimes years of silence or unintelligible prattle. She stood holding the two hands, forming a link between the two whom she had grown to love so much.

'Hallo, David. Did you want something?' she asked, in a quietly conversational voice.

The child turned and pointed across the room to a low chest of drawers. His little face was contorted with an obvious effort of concentration.

'M ... my t ... t ... train,' he stuttered, looking back at her helplessly. Jane dropped gently to her knees, disengaging her hand from Duncan's vice-like grip.

'You want me to get it?' she asked.

The young lips moved and the chin quivered, but no words came.

'All right,' said Jane comfortingly, 'you show me where it is.'

The train was recovered and with a grateful grin David trotted off to join his playmates. Jane stood up and faced Duncan across the classroom. As their eyes met, her knees became weak. Suddenly she needed the support of the heaven-sent chest of drawers. He had crossed the room in a moment and by common consent they moved into the adjoining store-room where the children's books and toys were stacked on long shelves. As they stood together in silence among all the paraphernalia of childish play, the arm that had guided her through the doorway tightened about her waist.

'Thank you,' she breathed as she leant gratefully against his strong supporting form.

'Come now, Jane.' His voice was gentle but it betrayed that he too was feeling the emotional impact of the scene in the classroom.

'I . . . I'm so sorry,' muttered Jane, as she moved away from his encircling arm. 'It is always a terrific feeling, when they first speak I mean, but I've never done this before. Stupid . . . I'm sorry. I really am all right now.' With a determined lift of her chin, she turned to face him.

Duncan was smiling happily with an expression that she had never seen before — and yet, perhaps she had, once. She had a very clear memory of him saying 'You are a very nice person, Jane' as they stood in the library doorway in that far away time before she learned that he was not engaged to Teresa Ronelli.

'Thank you, Jane,' he said simply, and with a touching note of humility that caught at her heartstrings.

'It wasn't me,' she assured him. 'I haven't done anything.'

'Haven't you?' He grinned almost boyishly. 'Well then, I thank you in advance for what you are about to do; for what you will do for David — not to mention myself. It will be all right now, won't it?'

She smiled tremulously at this all-confident man who was now almost diffidently seeking her assurance.

'I can't promise anything.' She shook her head, and then added impulsively, 'But I think so, for what my opinion is worth.'

Duncan laughed a truly happy laugh. 'If it could be measured, it would be worth its weight in gold to me at this moment,' he said as he reopened the classroom door.

Jane returned to the children: Duncan to his round. The day continued in a glow of happiness for at least two people at the Villa Alto.

It was late in the day when Jane made her way to the library in response to a summons from Duncan. His secretary had finished her work for the day so Jane knocked gently on the heavy main door. In response to Duncan's voice she let herself into the room. He rose from the desk and crossed the room to meet her.

'Thank you for coming, Jane.' He indicated a pair of deep armchairs away from the desk. 'Shall we sit here?'

The question was rhetorical; he moved the chair slightly for her convenience. With heightened sensitivity to his every mood Jane realised that this solicitous attitude was not at all unusual in their working relationship. It was only when personal matters arose, matters outside their working relationship, that cold formality entered his attitude to her. His personal affairs so far as they concerned David were necessarily part of the child's medical history, and as such he was willing to share them with her. Beyond that a barrier

160

seemed to exist between them.

'Well?' he queried, as he settled into the chair opposite her own.

She had no need to ask what that query meant. Their minds were perfectly attuned in their work. As a doctor and his specialist assistant they functioned as a perfect team; only as man and woman did their relationship become difficult. Could it be, Jane asked herself, that while he recognised her ability to do her work he disliked to be reminded that she was a woman? After all, he had tried to force on her the status of a nurse rather than that of a specialist assistant in the early days at the clinic. Jane realised with a sense of surprise that she knew very little of Duncan's personal views on such matters. Perhaps he did resent her feminine presence in what he regarded as an exclusively masculine working world. And yet she found it hard to attribute such an unreasonable attitude to such an eminently reasonable man as Duncan Frobisher.

A movement from Duncan recalled her wandering thoughts. He was still waiting for her answer.

'How has the day progressed?' he asked.

'It has progressed, but not quite according to plan,' she replied thoughtfully. 'David is talking, but his anxiety to express himself is causing him to stutter more and more. I can see that it is worrying him not to be able to say the words that are in his mind now that he has decided to talk. The whole case is rather different from that of a deaf child who can't hear the odd sound of his voice when he first speaks.'

'Are you going to find it very worrying?' His tone was almost disinterested, but Jane had a clear vision of his face as it had been that morning and she knew that he was far more concerned than he cared to show.

'I wouldn't say that I am worried,' she replied, 'but I do feel very much on my own. I'd give a lot to hear Dr Hamilton-Ayres's opinion at this point.'

'Well, I think I can help you there. Let's have a word with him.' Duncan glanced at his watch. 'Yes, with any luck we should catch him at this time.'

At first Jane was at a loss to understand the meaning of these remarks, but as he crossed the room towards the telephone she realised Duncan's intention. While he was waiting for the call to be connected to London, he asked Jane whether she would like to speak to the elderly specialist herself, but she was only too happy to leave the two medical men to their own discussions and profit from their joint advice.

As luck would have it the call was put straight through to its destination and Jane listened to Duncan's clear, concise description of events since the night before. She was mildly surprised to hear his description of her suggested explanation of the sudden change in David and gratified to realise that both doctors considered it a very likely solution. Only at one point did Duncan's tone vary fractionally. 'No. I hardly think he does,' he answered, in reply to an unheard question. 'He claimed me at the beginning, but I am more inclined to think that it was as an adult male rather than as a particular person.'

The conversation went on, but Jane no longer consciously heard the words that were spoken. Obviously the question had been whether David had recognised Duncan as his father. Looking back on the day, Jane realised that the little boy had shown no memory of the night before nor made any attempt to approach Duncan. At last the telephone conversation seemed to be ending.

'Yes . . . No, not tomorrow. I don't leave here until the late flight . . . That's right . . . Certainly I will . . . Goodbye.'

Duncan recrossed the room to the chair opposite hers.

'Well, Jane. I'll try to give you a summary of what you were not able to hear.'

What he told her fitted so well with what she felt was right in David's case that Jane began to feel quite relaxed as confidence returned to reinforce her own ideas. Duncan finished the detailed discussion and continued into generalities.

'H.A. suggests that it would not be wise to act precipitatively. Incidentally, he asked me to tell you that he never forgets a star pupil and that he has every confidence in your judgement. That is praise indeed from the Old Man. Now, where was I? Oh, yes. He suggests that as David doesn't seem to recognise me yet, there is no need to keep him with me when I leave for London tomorrow.'

This last was news indeed to Jane. Obviously this part of the conversation had taken place while her attention was wandering elsewhere.

Duncan continued slowly. 'H.A. thinks that it would be better for the child to remain here in the surroundings that he knows and gain confidence. If it is necessary, another trip will have to be made at a later date to take David to London.' After a pause he asked quietly, 'Does any of that make you feel any better?'

'Yes.' Jane replied simply. Then with more feeling she added, 'Yes, it does. It fits in with my own feelings so well that it is a great relief.'

'Well, I'm glad of that. I'm sorry to have to leave just at this time, but my visit to London is rather urgent. I don't want to cancel it if it can be avoided.'

Their conversation was cut short at this point by a call for Duncan from one of the wards.

* * *

It turned out on the following day that Max and Mario were to be jointly responsible for the running of the clinic while Duncan was away.

Jane had no opportunity to see Duncan again before he left but she did receive a brief note from him giving two telephone numbers at which she would be able to contact him, and urging her not to hesitate if she felt the need to get in touch with him.

The nursing staff continued in their unchangeable routine and for Jane a comfortable calm settled over the Villa Alto. The days took on the same pleasant atmosphere that had characterised her early weeks at the clinic. The summer was at its height and the days were long and hot. From their mountain top the lake looked cool and inviting, but in reality the valley below was unbearably hot and airless in comparison with their higher position. When Jane ventured down the mountainside for an afternoon with Dorothy Archer, the two girls found that the lake water was too warm for their long-anticipated swim to be enjoyably refreshing.

When Mario heard of her experience in the valley he laughed at her lack of wisdom and promised to show her some of the surrounding countryside in the cool of the evenings. So it was that very soon it became the accepted order of things that Mario should be seen on many evenings driving with Jane, or sipping a refreshing drink with her on the terrace of any one of the many hotels on the shores of the lake. On these outings they were often accompanied by Teresa who was anxious to improve her knowledge of the English language in conversation with Jane. At other times Jane and Mario explored the country-side alone. She found him a pleasantly undemanding companion, with an ability to make her feel very full of youth and spontaneous gaiety.

Max could not take part in these excursions because it was necessary for him to stay at the clinic if Mario was away. On the days when Mario stayed to set Max free, Jane felt that it was only fair to allow the engaged couple to spend their time alone. In spite of repeated invitations from both Max and Teresa, she steadfastly refused to spend her evenings with them.

During this time the two girls came to know each other and Jane found that she liked the Italian girl more and more. Teresa in her turn showed by many small gestures an increasing liking for her new English friend. The three of them returned one evening to find Max rather perturbed and anxious to speak to Jane alone. She went with him to the familiar library.

'I'm sorry, Jane, but it seems that old Duncan is a bit put out with us,' Max told her as soon as they were alone. 'Tonight is the third time that he has been on the phone and asked for you while you were out.'

'Oh, Max!' she exclaimed in horror. 'Why didn't you tell me about the other times?'

'Well, you know Duncan. He just asked casually if you were about, and then said it wasn't important anyway. I've told him what I could about David and he seemed happy enough till tonight.'

'What did he say, Max?' she asked fearfully.

'Blew his top completely, I'm afraid. Asked what Mario thought he was doing, gallivanting off with you, and what the blazes I was doing to let you go. I need hardly add that Duncan in that mood is not a man to have a discussion with.' Max was obviously depressed by his brother's disapproval.

'Oh dear,' sighed Jane. 'I have rather asked for it, haven't I? I might have guessed that Duncan would want to speak to me about David. To find me missing three times in a row is enough to annoy him. I can understand that.'

'Now look here, Jane.' It was Max's turn to speak with annoyance. 'There is no need whatever for you to take that attitude. Duncan is the one who is wrong and I told him so tonight. I told him he couldn't expect you to spend your free time sitting waiting for him to telephone.'

'Oh, Max! You shouldn't have said that,' she expostulated.

'What on earth did he say?'

'He didn't,' replied Max grimly. 'He simply rang off.'

The incident upset Jane considerably; particularly because she felt that she had let Duncan down. She had no idea what had made it necessary for him to be in London but she did know that he regretted parting from his son at this time. She could have bridged the gap more surely than anyone else, if only she had been there ready and waiting to reassure him . . .

But he did not telephone in the evening again. Over the following few days, she gathered, from conversations between the staff, that a few calls had been received from him during the daytime — all of which happened to coincide with her busiest periods of work, and none of which included any request to speak to her.

Although Jane did come very close to dialling the number at which Duncan had said he could be reached, some instinctive feminine caution stayed her hand. After spending three consecutive evenings at the villa in fruitless waiting, she gave herself a firm talking-to, determined to put it out of her mind, and accepted Mario's invitation to take advantage of the glorious sunshine to conduct a further exploration of the lakeside.

That evening, after the pair had spent a thoroughly enjoyable afternoon motoring around the lake — interposed with refreshment stops to sample the local *gelato* — she returned to the Villa Alto in a decidedly sprightly frame of mind. Having waved Mario gaily off to the cheerful toot of his horn, Jane was beginning to mount the staircase when she was waylaid by one of the Italian maids, who informed her that Dr Frobisher had expressed a wish to see Signorina Marten in the library upon her return.

Duncan must have telephoned again — and on her first evening out in days! Thanking the maid, and with spirits only slightly dampened by the prospect of another private conference with Max concerning his brother's ill-timed communications, Jane retraced her route down the stairs, crossed the hallway into the library — and stopped dead at the arresting sight of that familiar commanding presence seated at the desk, for this was not the Dr Frobisher she had been expecting.

'But — I thought you weren't back until — '

'So I see,' he said coolly, noting her air of surprise. 'I elected to take an earlier flight. I did telephone ahead to ensure news of my changed schedule reached the staff — all who were here to be reached, that is.'

Jane felt herself bridle slightly with annoyance at this, but reined in the retort which sprang to her lips, opting instead for a steady, 'I hope your visit went well.'

'Perfectly, thank you.' His eyes travelled contemplatively over the sprightly ribbon in her hair, the healthy flush to her cheeks, and the sparkle to her eyes which even the shock of his presence had not quite succeeded in damping. 'As did your outing today, I hope. I gather you have been rather enjoying yourself of late.'

Had that been an involuntary flash of

appreciation in Duncan's eyes, there and gone in an instant before he collected himself? Yes, she was sure. Suppressing a slight smile, Jane sidestepped his insinuation and opted instead for a demure, 'I was told you wanted to see me.'

'Whilst Matron has assured me that the children are well and happy, I do naturally expect more detailed reports on their progress during my absence.'

'Of course.' She smoothed down her skirt, sifting through the past few days' developments in her mind. 'David has — '

'Unless there is something of particular urgency to impart, I think it can wait until tomorrow, don't you?'

'If you would prefer.'

'I would.' Duncan steepled his fingers and fixed her with his gaze. 'I will see you in the library tomorrow for a full account. I'm afraid that, in light of this, any plans for further excursions with Mario tomorrow will have to be postponed.'

'Oh, he understands quite well that

my duties here must take priority over leisure. He has proved himself a splendid friend.' A little imp of mischief prompted her to add: 'It has been very pleasant, spending time with a man so . . . straightforward.'

'Indeed.' His eyebrows flicked upwards briefly. 'I only hope that such an excess of straightforwardness has not been too . . . tedious an experience for you.'

'On the contrary,' she countered lightly, 'I found my past several days of *gallivanting*, as I believe you put it, immensely fulfilling. Mario has been delightful company, and I find that the change has agreed with me. I must have been getting very dull.'

But she had never yet won a verbal round with Duncan.

'While Mario is teaching you not to be dull, I suggest that he also teaches you a little respect for your elders and betters, young woman. We shall meet again in the morning. Now off you go to bed.'

Having reduced her to the status of

an erring child he turned and the library door closed firmly before Jane could summon an answering retort. So he had defeated her again! But nothing could quell her high spirits that night. There was a song in her heart as she ran lightly to her room. Her last waking thought was of that momentary look of awareness for herself that she had seen in Duncan Frobisher's eyes.

Jane's interview with Duncan came earlier in the day than she was prepared for. When his secretary asked her if she could arrange to make her report immediately after the morning class, Jane knew that she had visualised this meeting quite differently. Unconsciously she had built up a picture in which he would take the reports of the other staff throughout the day, leaving herself until the last so that they would meet in the evening when the day's work was finished for both of them. It had seemed inevitable that Duncan would leave anything which concerned himself personally until the end of the day.

Now a nagging doubt crept into her mind. Was Duncan somehow aware of her desire for this more personal approach? Had he deliberately timed their meeting to point out that her position was no different from that of any other member of the staff, in spite of her special contact with David?

If she had any doubts about the tone of the interview they were dispelled as soon as she entered the library. He was seated as usual at the great desk in front of the terrace windows. Beside him, notebook in hand, sat his secretary. He rose to greet her with the formal politeness that was to characterise the whole interview. He was unmistakably the medical superintendent receiving a report from a member of his staff — no more, and certainly no less. They discussed the progress of the four children left in Jane's care. She gave him a brief report on each child and that was all. Not even a detectable flicker of increased interest showed in his grey eyes as she mentioned David's name. For that interview David was just another patient of the clinic. Duncan expressed neither approval nor disapproval of her work, which he appeared to take for granted; just as he seemed to take herself for granted, Jane thought, with a wry inward smile.

Eventually she found herself outside the library doors again with the realisation that not a personal word or reference had passed between them. So formal in fact had been that meeting that she was quite convinced that she would be called back to the library later in the day. Of course, she told herself, she had been right in her first judgement. Duncan Frobisher would not turn his mind to his personal affairs and David until he had once again taken over every detail of the administration of the clinic. He was a man who would always put duty first, Jane told herself. The description 'cold-hearted' slipped unwelcomely into her mind. Angrily she was forced to admit that the thought was prompted by her own disappointment at his lack of gratifying enthusiasm for her report of David's not inconsiderable improvement. Impatiently she brushed aside such thoughts and waited for the call to a second and more personal meeting with David's father.

The day wore slowly to its end without the expected summons to the library and slowly the earlier thoughts returned, unbidden, to Jane's mind. She could not help thinking that Duncan Frobisher was altogether too self-controlled, too discreet. To regard the well-being of his son in this apparently academic light was something that Jane's warm and tender heart found hard to understand — hard to forgive. But in her more honest moments she knew quite well that her disappointment was not all on David's behalf. Since the instant of meeting in the hall on the night before, Jane had lived with a glorious hope. Something had passed between them across the silence that was new and infinitely exciting: something that even to herself she hardly dared to admit.

Jane slept that night with disillusion as an unwelcome companion.

It was late in the following day before the expected summons to the library came. Jane was tired and dispirited, and in no mood to hold her own with Duncan if any difficulty should arise. She decided to postpone the difficult task of discussing her own future and to keep carefully to the subject of David's progress.

The fates did not seem in favour of Jane that day. Although she talked carefully of David, there was an uneasy atmosphere in the room and she felt that Duncan was somehow withdrawn and distant from herself; almost as though he were standing back to appraise her in some new light. This was so different from the usual careful attention that he gave to her work that Jane found herself speaking hesitantly and once even colouring uncontrollably as their eyes met. But Duncan appeared not to notice her discomfiture. Eventually he got up from his desk and strolled towards the open windows.

'And now,' he said, 'I would like to hear what you have to say about something that has arisen while I was away.'

'Yes?' she responded, wondering unhappily what was to come next.

It appeared that the parents of her two ex-pupils had paid her the compliment of wanting to return the children to her care. Both were English children but one had been exceptionally difficult to teach.

'They were so impressed with the progress of their offspring,' Duncan told her, 'that they are determined to retain your services, if possible. I have explained,' he continued, 'that you are not permanently at the disposal of the clinic, but they are quite willing to pay your full salary between them if you will take on their infants.'

He turned to her and smiled. If he had been anyone but Duncan Frobisher she would have described the smile as diffident. He was looking at her with the first hint of embarrassment that she had ever known him to show.

'I am not very good at making complimentary speeches, Jane. I can only say that I would be more than willing to join in the scheme and so keep David with you for as long as possible.'

Jane stared at him unbelievingly and all her irritation of the previous day fell away. This was the smiling, friendly Duncan whom she found it most difficult to face with a calm exterior.

'Where would you want me to work?' she asked carefully.

His eyes narrowed and his voice had lost its previous warmth when he spoke.

'Mario said that would be the stumbling block.'

'Mario?' she queried with surprise.

'Yes.' He paused, and then continued in the impersonal tone to which she had been accustomed for so long. 'Because of circumstances which need not concern you at present, I had to consult both Max and Mario about this scheme. I had taken it for granted that the best place would be here, in the clinic. Max was all in favour of the idea, but Mario was of the opinion that you would be happier away from the Villa Alto.'

'I see. What exactly did Mario say?' She asked the question nervously, fearing the answer and yet driven to ask by a compelling need to know what Duncan knew of her own affairs.

'You need not worry, Jane.' His voice was suave and faintly patronising. 'He merely implied that you might not wish to remain here for personal reasons.' That at least was reassuring. 'Whatever secret confidences Mario may have received remain your secret so far as *he* is concerned.'

The unmistakable emphasis in his last remark brought Jane's head up sharply to scan his face for an explanation, but none was forthcoming. She could not interpret his inscrutable expression.

'What do you mean — as far as *he* is concerned?' she asked.

Duncan made an impatient gesture and turned to face her. 'My dear Jane. If there is one thing I deplore it is people who get their emotions mixed up with their work. I am well aware of your difficulties here so far as that is concerned and I believe I have already congratulated you on the way that you have handled the situation.'

Jane stared at him in apprehensive bewilderment.

'I'm afraid I just don't understand what you are talking about,' she protested. The only explanation that presented itself could not possibly fit the situation. If Duncan had guessed her true feelings, surely nothing would induce him to drag them so cruelly before her. No, indeed she did not understand.

'Very well, Jane,' his tone was now unmistakably censorious. 'I thought that you had more sense, but as you seem determined to cause us both considerable embarrassment, I may as well tell you that I am giving you the opportunity to continue your work away from the disturbing atmosphere that you must find here because of your attachment to my brother.'

Genuine astonishment was swiftly followed by relief as she gazed unbelievingly at Duncan's sternly set face. A sound that was half a sob and half a laugh escaped her.

'My attachment to Max!' she exclaimed incredulously.

Duncan was obviously puzzled by her reaction, but his voice was unwaveringly stern. 'You must think me very insensitive if you believe that I was not aware of your difficulties. I am afraid that you let it become rather obvious at one time.'

She could not see his face as he stood looking out across the terrace but she was sure that it had softened as he tried to moderate criticism with kindness.

'But I . . . I . . . Oh, this is ridiculous!' she exclaimed. 'Of course I like Max, and Teresa,' she added with emphasis that was not lost on her audience. 'They are both delightful people. But to suggest that I . . . Well, I supose that you are suggesting that I have fallen for Max, to use a schoolgirl expression.'

'And haven't you?' he asked quietly without turning from the window.

'Of course not,' she replied vehemently.

Abandoning his careful inspection of the world outside the window Duncan turned his attention to her and watched her narrowly for a minute before he returned to his desk with a dismissive gesture that contrived to suggest the complete erasing of their previous conversation.

'We seem to have strayed a long way from our original subject. I would like you to think over the possibility that I have suggested to you, taking it for granted that you could work somewhere other than at the Villa Alto if you wished.'

6

'Thank you. Yes, I would like to think about it.'

'Very well, Jane. I shall not keep you now. Let me know your decision as soon as possible.' Duncan had the greatest facility for terminating any interview finally and irrevocably, so that the other person found themselves on the far side of a closed door before there was time to wonder if there was anything else to be said.

Jane's life stretched out before her as emptily as the marbled hallway outside the library door. She longed for just one good friend to whom she could pour out all her troubles. Instinctively her thoughts turned to Mario, but a certain reticence forbade her to seek him out. There was of course Mary Mackinlay, but Mac was far too closely associated with the Frobisher brothers for this particular sort of confiding. She had never been more lonely in her life than she was as she made her way back to the classroom to prepare work for the next day.

It was almost dark by the time that she had finished her work for the day, but the air was very warm and still. Gratefully she stepped out into the cooler air of the garden and sought her favourite seat overlooking the lake, outlined by a string of lights, far below.

Jane had never faced a more difficult decision than the one before her now. She knew that the personal tuition of the children without interference from any ruling school authority would be very satisfactory to her. It would be a welcome task if it were not for the complication of little David. The child would very soon outgrow the stage at which she could be useful to him; in a few months at the most she could sever all connection with the Villa Alto clinic and the Frobisher family if she wished. In the meantime, however, it was unthinkable to insist on parting the child from his father without a very good reason, and what reason could she offer to Duncan Frobisher? It seemed that if she was to accept the responsibility of teaching these three children her life would be inevitably bound to the clinic for months to come. The idea at once thrilled and dismayed her.

As she sat, trying to settle the chaotic thoughts that Duncan's return and its sequel had brought, the sound of footsteps behind her made her turn. Through the gathering darkness she could make out a masculine figure advancing towards her — too tall and broad for Mario — none of the porters would be about so late. As the tall figure strolled slowly nearer, she knew that it was one of the Frobisher brothers. A sense of inescapable nearness told her that it was Duncan long before she could make out the minute details of features that distinguished the brothers.

'Not sightseeing tonight?' he enquired conversationally. He stood looking down at her with a quizzical amusement which contrasted strangely with the grim expression which she had seen on his face only a few hours before.

'Strictly the answer is — No,' she replied, 'but in fact I suppose I am. This is sightseeing enough for me.' She indicated the valley below.

'Just so,' he remarked enigmatically.

Together they contemplated the scene below in silence.

'Am I disturbing the bliss of solitude?' he enquired, after a long pause.

Even in the darkness she knew that the curious half-smile which had the power to set her heart beating faster was lurking in his eyes. He obviously had no intention of referring to their earlier conversation.

'In vacant or in pensive mood',' she quoted, and then laughed uncertainly. 'I suppose I was.'

'I wonder what Wordsworth would have made of this scene,' he mused.

She watched him curiously as he gazed down on the scene before them.

This was Duncan in a mood that she did not know. She had never known anyone, Jane reflected, who was able to divide their life into two such definite parts as Duncan Frobisher.

'Have you fallen in love with Italy, Jane?' he asked suddenly.

She considered the unexpected question carefully.

'I wouldn't say that I have fallen in love,' she said, 'but I do admit to infatuation.'

'You know the difference?' His tone matched his strange expression so that she was not sure whether he was laughing at her or not.

Jane was grateful for the darkness which hid the blush that she could not control until a match suddenly flared as he applied it to his pipe. They were regarding each other across an island of light. With a determined effort, Jane laughed vivaciously.

'Wordsworth had something to say about love of country too,' she countered.

'What in particular?' he asked quietly.

She found that she had no self-consciousness in quoting the well-known lines to him.

"'I travell'd among unknown men,
In lands across the sea;
Nor, England! did I know till then
What love I bore to thee.''

'And have you Wordsworth's reason?' His words cut across the stillness that followed her quotation.

'His reason?' she repeated uncomprehendingly.

'Surely you know the last verse too?' He took his pipe from his mouth and leant against the balustrade of the terrace.

"'Thy mornings showed, thy nights conceal'd
The bowers where Lucy play'd;
And thine too is the last green field
That Lucy's eyes survey'd.''

His voice was low and vibrant as he spoke the simply moving words.

'Is there a Lucy in England for you, Jane?' he asked.

She permitted herself an upward glance at him, but he was again looking away from her into the darkness.

'I didn't choose a very apt quotation, did I?' she asked nervously. She had attempted to turn the conversation from the personal to the general and only succeeded in bringing it still closer to the subject that she most wished to avoid.

'That depends on what you wanted to convey,' he told her. 'If, for instance, you wanted to tell me that there is someone in England who can claim your love from the infatuation of Italy, then the verse was very aptly chosen indeed.'

'But I didn't!' she protested, and immediately regretted the vehemence of her response to his hidden question. 'I simply meant that although Italy is very beautiful, England still has a charm which, to me at least, gives it a greater claim to my affection.'

'I see,' he said. 'I think I agree with you.' He drew on his pipe thoughtfully for a moment and then offered his hand to her. The gesture held all the command of his dominant personality and Jane found her hand in his before she was aware of any conscious action.

More under the influence of his will than of her own she found herself standing in front of him. They were so close that she could feel the warmth of his breath in her hair, and still he did not release her imprisoned hand.

'You are really amazingly small, Miss Marten.' There was a note of amused surprise and a hint of pleasure in his deep voice.

'Do I usually appear so very large then?' she asked, with a breathless attempt at laughter.

His free hand tilted her chin until their eyes met.

'Alarmingly so sometimes,' he told her. His voice was serious but amusement played in the grey eyes that met hers. Jane found that she could laugh too as he turned and led her slowly across the terrace. Her hand within his thrilled warmly to the contact. As they neared the open doorway, he raised her arm and regarded their clasped hands attentively.

'I thought only children could be as small as that,' he said, with the same note of surprised amusement as before. With which somewhat clinical observation he released her hand and raised his own in salute.

'Goodnight, Jane.'

He was gone, into the darkness, before she could reply.

The inconsistency of the intimacy of their conversation on the terrace and the sudden parting left Jane bewildered and hurt. Parting from Duncan was always swift and decisive; she was used to that. It was the sense of incompleteness that made her quiet and thoughtful for the rest of that evening.

In the past weeks Duncan's concern for his little son had broken through much of his habitual reserve and allowed her to see beneath his stern self-control in brief glimpses. Inevitably a closer relationship had grown between them as they watched the child's progress. Was it, she asked herself, that bond alone that had prompted him to put aside his usual taciturn exterior and reveal a little of his true personality to her? In the answer to that question lay the key to Jane's happiness. Wistfully she wondered if she would ever really get to know this unpredictable man who had the power to stir her emotions so strongly.

It was with some surprise that Jane received a call to the library on the following day. She had not been able to settle her thoughts after the disturbing events of the previous day and had come no nearer to the decision which she expected Duncan to ask for. In spite of her persistent indecision it was in a mood of happy anticipation that she gathered her files together and made her way to the library; confident in the belief that, at least in her work, she had established a new and satisfactory relationship with Duncan.

Some of her confidence evaporated as she faced him across his desk. There was none of the smiling unpredictable Duncan of the evening before in the medical superintendent of the morning. He rose as she entered the room, but his face did not vary from its usual withdrawn expression as he motioned her to sit down.

'You wanted to see me?' she asked.

He nodded, without any change of expression.

'Yes, I did. But you can put those files away. It is not about them that I want to speak to you. I want to ask you to do something.'

'Yes?'

'Will you take David to England for me, tomorrow?'

'Tomorrow?' she repeated dazedly.

His expression did not alter as he met her surprised stare. 'Will you?' he demanded, almost fiercely.

'Of course, if you think it is urgent,

but he seems very well to me.'

'I am glad to be able to say that I agree with you, but I want you to take him to my sister as soon as possible.'

'To Mrs Gresham? I don't understand.'

'He seems to have no memory of myself, but he may remember the places and people where he has spent most of his life.' There was a hint of weariness in his tone, but Jane was too preoccupied to notice it.

'Yes, I can see that, but I still don't understand the urgency, why it should be tomorrow.'

'I should have thought it would have been patently obvious to you, Jane. I have told you that I abhor people who allow their emotions to become mixed with their working life. And before you tell me that you don't understand what I mean,' he continued purposefully, 'just answer one question.' He paused momentarily. 'Will you go to England and take David with you tomorrow?'

So that was it! In spite of all her

attempts to hide her emotional turmoil he had detected her feelings and she was being dismissed from his carefully ordered life. There was no place for a love-sick woman in Duncan Frobisher's self-sufficient existence. Jane felt humiliated, and resentful. Had she looked up to meet his eyes she might have doubted her own conclusions, but she was beyond the control of her usual level-headed judgement.

Her voice was cold and small with anger as she put her own interpretation on his words.

'If you want me to go, you don't have to make the excuse of sending David with me.'

'Jane!' he exclaimed roughly. 'Please stop pretending to be stupid. Will you or will you not take David to my sister?'

'Why?' Her small head lifted defiantly.

'Because I ask you to, and the child needs the security of a known person in a changed environment.'

'And what after I have delivered him?'

Duncan made an impatient gesture.

'There is no question of delivering him. I shall expect you to stay with him. My sister is already expecting you.'

'I see,' she said coldly. 'And how long am I to remain with the Greshams?'

'Until you hear otherwise from me.'

'Have you any idea when that is likely to be?' she enquired icily.

'No. I can't say that I have at present.' His urbane manner infuriated her, but whatever else might have been said was cut short by the entrance of his secretary.

Duncan used the opportunity characteristically.

'Thank you, Miss Marten,' he said formally. 'I am very grateful for your cooperation. I hope you'll have a pleasant journey and that young David will give you no cause for concern.'

Jane left the room as there was obviously no point in attempting to continue the discussion at that time, but she had by no means had her full say on the subject. She was determined to seek a further interview with Duncan later in the day. He apparently intended to unceremoniously terminate her engagement at the clinic and pack her off to England like some badly behaved child being sent home from a treat.

Well this was one time when Duncan Frobisher would not find everything going his own way, Jane told herself grimly. Nor was she any more pleased with the situation when, later in the day, she learned that Duncan had left the clinic for a visit to Milan and was not expected to return for three days.

All the arrangements had been made for her journey by his secretary and there was nothing left for Jane to do but to pack a few necessary items and go. Much as she would have liked to defy his orders and remain until he returned, she could not bring herself to do so.

Although nobody but Mary Mackinlay knew David's true identity, every member of the clinic staff was aware of the events of the past few weeks and they were watching the child's progress with great interest. Jane found that too many people were already aware of the proposed journey for her to cancel it without inviting considerable comment.

Angry tears clouded her vision as she packed one small suitcase ready for the flight. Why? Why, she demanded of herself, did he have to add to her humiliation by sending David with her? At least he could have let her go without the added insult of having to meet him again.

David accepted the news of the coming journey with the easy philosophy of the very young. As they drove to the airport in the hired car, Jane had little time for her own thoughts. Her small companion chattered gaily, apparently quite unaware of the fact that she could not understand more than half his words as they tumbled out in an incomprehensible mixture of syllables.

She had avoided saying goodbye to most of the staff, who in any case believed that she would return as soon as David was safely deposited in

England, but she had been unable to leave without at least some word to Mary Mackinlay. To Mac alone she intimated that it might be longer than most people expected before her return to the Villa Alto. Mac, with her usual shrewd perspicacity, knew without further words that Jane was desperately unhappy, but with characteristically tactful kindness she asked no questions. Her only request was that Jane should write to her from England and let her know how the future worked out.

'The future!' thought Jane bitterly. What could she make of the future after the abysmal mess that she had made of the past?

The airport provided great excitement for David, which he indulged with unsophisticated abandon. Every aspect of the plane needed examination and explanation and the restraint of his safety belt was almost more than the little boy could bear.

When at last they were fully airborne, the boredom of unrelieved cloud soon brought its sleepy reaction. With a winning smile he curled his small body onto Jane's lap and slept with the same babyish thoroughness that he brought to his every activity. As she looked down at the sleeping child, Jane was deeply moved by his absolute trust. Once or twice she put her cheek against the dark, curly hair. Tears came silently to her eyes and she vowed inwardly that in spite of Duncan, but never for him, she would do all in her power to retain and strengthen that moving trust.

★ ★ ★

Celia Gresham had apparently contacted Jane's parents and it was already arranged that they should all meet on the following day, but the first evening was devoted to settling David into his new surroundings.

Jane noticed with considerable surprise the natural and unsensational manner in which Celia dealt with David's speech difficulty. She realised that behind the poise and beauty of the other woman there was an understanding and warm human sympathy which sprang from the difficulties which she had experienced with her own little son's deafness. Suddenly Jane felt a warm liking for this sister of Duncan. Friendship began to grow between herself and this woman who previously had been no more than a pleasant acquaintance, met in the course of her work.

Tony Gresham was already in bed when the two travellers arrived and David was soon tucked up in the next room under the careful eye of an obviously capable nanny.

At dinner that night Jane found that she had to answer many questions about the well-being of Celia's twin brothers. Before the evening was through she was aware of a very close affection between the Frobisher family in which Celia's husband, Edward, obviously shared. It was clear that Edward Gresham held both his brothers-in-law in affectionate esteem, although Jane felt that she could detect a slight bias on his part in favour of Duncan.

By the time that the evening drew to a close, Jane realised that she had landed in a veritable bed of thorns despite the gracious peace of the household. There would be no escape from Duncan's all-powerful personality, while she remained in the Greshams' home.

In the days that followed, Jane became accepted by both Celia and Edward Gresham on easy and friendly terms. Although David showed no apparent memory of the house or the people in it, his speech improved noticeably under the influence of Tony Gresham's need to lip-read his words. The two children were happy to play at childish make-believe for hours on end. Jane withdrew as often as possible in the firm belief that they were proving better tutors for each other than she could ever hope to be from her elevated position in the world of grown-ups.

Her own sense of unhappiness and the still burning smart of Duncan's apparent gross injustice were lulled into uneasy quiescence and she knew that her sense of proportion was readjusting itself. She was even tempted to hope for a complete recovery of her old self-confidence before she had to face Duncan again.

They had been in England for a week when Celia Gresham invited Jane to join her for a day's outing. They were talking round a welcome fire after dinner when Celia made the suggestion. The evening was cool but only just cold enough to justify the cheerful fire that crackled in the grate.

'The children will be quite happy with Nanny,' Celia said, 'and I would like your help down at Ives.'

Jane, who had developed a great liking for Duncan's beautiful sister, was pleased at the suggestion that they should spend a full day together. She looked at the other woman enquiringly.

'I would love to come,' she said

truthfully. 'Where is Ives?'

'In Sussex,' Celia told her. 'Duncan asked me to go down and have a look when he was at home last month. He wants to get it open, ready for when he moves home from Italy.'

At the mention of his name, Jane's heart gave an uncomfortable lurch which told her that Duncan Frobisher still meant far more to her than she cared to admit, even to herself.

'Is he coming back to England then?' she enquired, carefully avoiding Celia's glance.

'I thought that you would know all about it,' said Celia. 'Hasn't he mentioned it in Italy?' she asked curiously.

'He probably has,' responded Jane quickly, 'but not to me. After all, it would hardly concern me.'

'No, I suppose not,' conceded Celia. 'And Duncan is not the world's most communicative mortal, is he?'

Jane laughed in spite of herself at this understated description of the most taciturn individual that it had ever been her misfortune to meet — 'much less to love', a nagging inward voice told her ruefully.

'All the same,' Celia seemed puzzled, 'I should have thought that he would have told you. After all, it affects David's future and Duncan obviously considers you an important person in that young man's life.'

Jane smiled wistfully as she wondered what Celia would say if she knew the real reason for the sudden journey to England for David and herself. Luckily no explanation had been necessary. The Greshams were content with Duncan's decree that the child should return to surroundings that might arouse his memory. Much as she would have liked to question Celia further, Jane could not bring herself to do so.

Edward Gresham rustled his newspaper and glanced over it at the two women.

'When you two have quite finished analysing my brother-in-law, perhaps you'll tell me what to expect by way of plans for tomorrow,' he suggested.

'Oh, yes, Ives of course — ' Celia dragged her mind back from consideration of Duncan's behaviour. 'I am sorry, Edward, but you know what I am like when I get down there. I get all reminiscent and I've no idea how the time passes.' She turned to Jane. 'Ives is our family home, Jane. Although it belongs to Duncan now, we all think of it as our ultimate home. I just can't explain to you how I love that place.' She finished dreamily and almost to herself.

Edward chuckled at his wife indulgently.

'You see how it is, Jane,' he said. 'I slave myself to a shadow for the ungrateful woman only to find that she is in love with a house.' The final word was emphasised with mock disgust.

'Poor Edward,' laughed Celia. 'But you really must see Ives for yourself, Jane. I think you will understand what I mean when you do. Oh, it's not one of the 'stately homes' or anything like that, but it is a very real part of history. The original house is Tudor and quite unspoilt. Even an addition in the days of the Georges has not spoilt the original character. In fact I sometimes think that the contrast has enhanced the attraction of the whole place. Edward agrees with me, don't you, darling?' she added.

'Celia, you know quite well that I have no choice. Ives to you is a belief, not a house at all; and who am I, a mere mortal, to disagree?'

He looked at Jane as she watched them from her position between the two. 'To tell you the truth, Jane, the old place is well worth a visit. Duncan is a lucky chap to be able to keep it at all in these days.'

'Thank goodness for that luck,' exclaimed Celia devoutly. 'The house is a sort of trust, Jane. Most of the land has gone to pay death duties and taxes long ago, but by some miracle of the law a rich Victorian ancestor managed to endow the house so that it is ours at least for our generation and probably the next as well. Unless the law changes that too,' she added a trifle sadly.

Jane had never before thought much about the effect of changing society on the owners of the smaller historic houses. She had seen many of the great mansions change hands to public bodies, but it had all seemed very remote from her own quietly comfortable life, just as had the great villas of Italy.

As she stood, the following day, on the flagged terrace of Ives, she thought wistfully of other terraces far away in the sunshine of Italy. Suddenly Duncan seemed very near as she looked at his home and out across the gently sloping meadow to a thread of river meandering through the fields below. The day was full of the mellow sunshine of late summer and the scene was so very much a part of England that Jane felt a lump rise in her throat as she stood there.

The house itself was every bit as charming as Celia had promised and the setting could not have been more perfect. Celia was right: this was something that belonged to the quiet, unsung part of a nation's history, and Jane shared her wish that it should continue so for many years to come.

While Celia went from room to room with the grey-headed housekeeper, Jane was free to wander as she pleased. She found much to interest her, but nothing more than the photographs of the three Frobishers in their youth. The two boys, even more startlingly alike then than now, seemed always together. The young Celia had always shown the promise of the beautiful woman that she was to become. A few portraits also claimed Jane's attention; particularly one of a woman who was obviously related to Celia although the deep-set grey eyes were those of the two boys in a neighbouring painting. As Jane stood in front of these portraits, Celia approached her, walking softly on the thickly carpeted floor.

'Do you think she was beautiful?' she asked, with more than usual softness in her voice.

'Very beautiful,' said Jane. 'You are like her,' she added shyly.

'I'm glad you think so.' Celia smiled happily. 'I couldn't want anything better than simply to be like her.'

'It is your mother?' Jane asked diffidently.

'Yes. She died when I was sixteen. Sometimes I almost seem to have forgotten her, and then I come here and see that portrait, and I know that I will never really forget her.'

Together they turned to look round the big drawing-room and faced another portrait of a very young woman, obviously of a more recent date.

'She is beautiful too,' said Jane, 'but in a different way.'

'Very different,' agreed Celia succinctly.

Puzzled at her companion's change of tone, Jane examined the portrait more closely. The girl was undoubtedly a beauty, but there was something disturbing about the picture. The glowing red hair fell loosely about an ivory-pale face. The head was held high with an uncomfortable arrogance that was confirmed by the blue eyes that looked into the room so vividly. The whole portrait was vibrantly alive, but no part more so than the hands. They were folded quietly enough on the girl's lap, but their stillness was that of arrested motion rather than peace. The extraordinarily long, bony fingers were curled in impatient immobility that was anything but restful.

Jane turned from the disturbing picture to find Celia watching her with interest and a hint of amusement.

'You don't like her?' Duncan's sister asked.

Jane shook her head. 'I don't think so,' she said. 'Should I?'

'I certainly did not,' said Celia emphatically. 'It doesn't matter now anyway.'

Without further words, Jane turned back to the portrait. She knew now, without doubt, that this was Duncan's dead wife. It was strange that a woman's child could bear so little resemblance to herself, Jane thought. There was no hint in David's cherubic features of his mother's vibrant beauty, although he showed such a strong resemblance to his father.

'It is a very fine portrait,' Jane said thoughtfully as she felt again the almost living impact of the dead girl's restless personality.

Celia's laugh had a bitter little ring.

'It was painted by a genius in love with his subject,' she said.

When Jane made no comment, Celia came to stand beside her.

'I hated her, Jane,' she said quietly. 'It is a long time ago and it doesn't matter now. She was beautiful, all right, but there never was a truer case of beauty being only skin deep. I think that she was the only big mistake that Duncan has ever made. It humbled him,' she finished simply.

The idea of Duncan being described by anyone as humble so startled Jane that she stared at his sister in amazement.

'Oh, I know what you're thinking,' said Celia with a short laugh. 'He doesn't give the impression of a humbled being,

I know. You have met him in his work, and heaven knows he has no particular grounds for humility there! But for his wife to run off with an artist — well, it is enough to humiliate any man who thought that he was in love with a deity.'

They turned away from the picture by common consent.

'It must be moved,' stated Celia in a matter-of-fact voice. 'There is a portrait of our grandmother that can be put in its place.'

Left alone while Celia went to give instructions for the changing of the portraits, Jane turned again to look at Duncan's wife. It was the hands which fascinated her more than the face. Avarice was so strongly expressed by those bony fingers that it filled the atmosphere around the picture. The artist might not have realised it but, even through the power of his love that had made the beautiful face so vivid, avarice was the emotion that he had expressed with such disturbing strength.

With a mental shake, Jane turned her

eyes to the view from the long windows. Two swans had settled on the winding river, their white plumage tinged with gold in the yellowing light of the early autumn evening. The desire to gain all this and Duncan for a husband was something that Jane could understand in any woman. To be discontented when it was all achieved was something beyond her comprehension. To callously throw it all away, and with it a baby son, was to Jane a sin which she could never forgive.

In those moments she realised that she was very close to Duncan in her thoughts. He was the one who had been sinned against — himself, his son and his beloved home. He had not forgiven. Jane wondered whether he had been to his home since his wife's death; whether he had looked at that portrait with unclouded eyes and seen the avarice in those hands.

As they drove home through the gathering darkness, Jane felt uncomfortable, as though she had taken an unfair advantage of Duncan Frobisher. She had lifted a veil of reserve and caught the real man unaware. Though why she should feel guilty when he had not hesitated to uncover her own secrets she did not know. The enigma of his taciturn exterior was to some extent clear to her now. She could have forgiven him so much if it had not been for that final mortifying scene, Jane told herself.

It was understandable that a man would be careful and suspicious in his dealings with his fellow men, and particularly women, after Duncan's experience. But to judge the whole of womankind by the standards of one faithless woman showed a cruelly unforgiving attitude to Jane's sensitive mind. He had not seen her growing love, of that she was confident, but by some strange instinct he had sensed it. It had been a cruel self-defence to treat her as he had, and argued a weakness of character which she could hardly credit to Duncan Frobisher.

The days went quietly by until Jane began to wonder if she would ever hear from Duncan again, except to receive her salary cheque, until young David no longer needed her care. But peace was not to last so long.

Edward Gresham had spent a few days away from home. He was expected to return in the early evening and the two children were allowed to stay up to greet him. There was much speculation as to whether there would be presents to be received, until the sound of the car cut short all but a frenzied rush for the door. Tony, who could not hear the car, started the race a little in the rear, but he beat his cousin to the front door by a short head.

As he struggled with the heavy door, Tony called out to anyone who would listen to him.

'Daddy. My Daddy is home. Come and meet my Daddy.'

With a shrill cry of delight he at last had the door open wide enough to permit his exit. By the time that Jane arrived on the scene her help was no longer needed and she and Celia laughed together at the eager little bundle that hurled itself at the parked car.

7

As they watched the joyful welcome, Jane became conscious of a small, hot hand seeking hers. She looked down to find David gazing up at her with wide, frightened eyes. She dropped on her knees beside him and took the little boy into her arms.

'What is the matter, David?' she asked, in as normal a voice as she could muster. Instinctively she held up a hand to warn the onlookers not to speak while the child gazed wonderingly about him, as if seeing his surroundings for the first time.

'Will *my* Daddy come?' he asked tearfully.

Jane's mouth was suddenly dry and there was an uncomfortable lump in her throat.

Before she could answer, a familiar voice above her head spoke quietly.

'Can I help?'

Jane looked up with startled recognition and the child in her arms struggled violently to free himself. Whimpering like a delighted puppy, David threw himself against the trousered legs beside them. No two people had ever been so pleased to see Duncan Frobisher.

To Jane his arrival seemed a miraculous descent from heaven. She rose from her knees and watched the little boy hoisted on to the strong broad shoulders of his father. This time there was no doubt about David's memory. The key that had locked his mind for so long had turned and light was flooding back as he crowed with almost hysterical delight in his new-found happiness.

Jane would willingly have left the family without her presence for the evening, but the Greshams would not allow her to go, and Duncan stood by with a mocking smile at her protests which in no way helped her to withdraw from his company gracefully. The celebratory atmosphere brought to the house by

Duncan's home-coming and David's demonstration was infectious so that Jane found herself drawn into the general pleasure to the family despite Duncan's disturbing presence.

She was determined not to be caught in the embarrassing situation of finding herself alone with him. All the time that she could count on the continued presence of a third person Jane knew that she would be able to maintain a façade of formal politeness. To the Greshams, who knew nothing of their earlier relationship, it would not seem at all strange to see her in the role of a deferentially friendly employee. As the evening wore on, her chosen part became increasingly difficult to maintain as she found Duncan regarding her on frequent occasions with an air of frankly puzzled amusement. He appeared to be thoroughly enjoying her discomfort and taking an amused interest in her handling of the situation.

When at last they all decided that it was time for bed, Jane and Celia rose together, but Duncan detained them with a gesture.

'I want a word with Jane,' he stated firmly. 'We'll follow you in a few minutes, if you don't mind.'

'Do you mind if we leave it until tomorrow?' asked Jane, her voice husky as she strove to conceal her panic.

'Why?' he enquired, with a quizzical smile.

Jane's latent anger boiled. How dare he put her in this position where she had to openly defy him or tamely submit to his will! Why did she have to love this man against her every inclination?

'I am rather tired,' she told him, but she could not keep a note of asperity from her voice and the look of startled surprise in Celia's eyes decided her that she must give way with at least apparent grace if he persisted.

'There really isn't much to tell you.' She spoke in a flat voice that disguised her anger. She hated him to know how easily he could rouse and embarrass her.

'Then it won't take very long to tell,' he asserted, with calm determination.

'Very well,' she assented with as much apparent grace as she could muster. She sat down again as Celia and Edward left the room and immediately regretted the move. It gave him an uncomfortable advantage, though she fiercely denied him any other superiority than that of height.

When they were alone, he turned to her with the smile that had the power to melt her heart.

'Well, Jane, is this grand act strictly necessary?' he asked.

'Do you wish me to let the Greshams know exactly how I feel about you?' she enquired coldly.

A puzzled frown appeared to replace the smile.

'I don't see why not.'

All Jane's hitherto controlled anger boiled up and spilled over in one explosive gesture as she sprang up from her chair.

'After our last interview, you can

hardly expect me to be polite to you for more than this one evening,' she exclaimed bitterly.

She turned to leave the room, but his hand fell heavily on her arm and her angry eyes met his frankly surprised stare.

'And what did I say at our last *interview* to bring about this reaction?' he enquired, regarding her intently.

'I should hardly think that it would be necessary to refresh your memory,' she retorted, meeting his gaze with angry resentment.

With compelling force, he thrust her unceremoniously back into her recently vacated chair.

'Now we shall get this straight,' he stated with determination.

'How dare you!' Her anger was dangerously near to tears.

'I'll dare a lot more if we don't get this straightened out,' he told her darkly. 'Now just tell me what I said to upset you so much.'

'I suppose you find it surprising that

I should dislike being told that, to quote your own words, you 'abhor people who allow their emotions to become mixed with their working life'.' Her head was high and her eyes still bright with anger, but she knew that it would not be long before she broke down before his keen gaze that seemed, as always, to burn into her soul. In that moment she believed that she hated him passionately.

Strangely it was Duncan who suddenly dropped his gaze. He sat down in the chair beside her own and spoke without looking at her.

'And to whose emotions did you think I was referring in that particular context?' His voice was curiously soft and kind.

She could find no voice to answer him.

'To yours I presume?' The statement was spoken with the inflection of a question. This time he waited for her to answer.

'Naturally,' she replied, a sudden

doubt entering her mind. There was a long silence in which neither looked at the other.

It was Duncan who spoke at last.

'You don't know me very well at all, do you Jane?' he asked.

She glanced curiously at him, but offered no reply.

'You were quite right in the first place,' he continued. 'It is too late to begin what must be a very long discussion. But take this one thought to bed with you and sleep on it well.' He stood up and raised her out of her chair so that they stood very close together. It took a lot of courage for Jane to raise her eyes to meet his. 'I am not quite the monster that you obviously think me,' he said quietly. 'Your emotions, Jane, would be as sacred to me as my own in any case, but particularly so in the present circumstances. I thought that you already knew that without being told, but it seems that I was wrong.'

She searched his face for some expression to amplify his words but she could not read what she saw, nor could she bring herself to look more deeply into those all-seeing grey eyes.

Gently he propelled her towards the door.

'Think of Wordsworth,' he suggested softly as she turned to close the door.

Again she looked to him for an explanation, but his attention was apparently concentrated on filling his pipe. He did not even glance at her. She realised that once again she was being swept into the emotional chaos that seemed to be inevitable in all her association with this unpredictable man.

The days that followed Duncan's arrival were quiet and uneventful. Now that David was well established and happy with Tony's nanny, Jane had arranged to sleep at her own home and spend the days at the Greshams' house where she continued to give lessons to both boys. In this way she avoided contact with Duncan, who was away from the house during the day, but her real problem was not solved. Everyone seemed to take her presence for granted and, so far as she could see, there was no immediate likelihood of an end to her association with Duncan's family. Daily she resolved to tell him that she felt her work with David was done and that she must look for other employ-ment. Such resolutions were easy to make but not so simple to put into effect. She found the days slipping by while she drifted uncertainly along in the new routine.

The autumn weather was already beginning to keep the children indoors on most days, and it was not surprising that both small boys became fractious at the enforced enclosure, even in the Greshams' large house.

It was with relief that Celia and Jane saw the sun filtering, at first weakly and then with increased warmth, into the gar-den on Nanny's day off. While the boys scampered happily at some game of great imagination and activity, Jane sat with Celia on a sun-warmed seat and felt relaxed and happy in the too-rare outdoor warmth.

They chattered idly about the children for a while and then launched into an entirely feminine discussion of the latest fashions. For all Celia's wealth, Jane found her unexpectedly conservative in matters of extreme fashion. The conversation had a delightful intimacy which was only interrupted by the return of the children, each carrying a load of leaves which represented unspecified imaginary merchandise.

8

'All for you, Mummy,' announced Tony, depositing his burden at his mother's feet.

David's sense of fair play did not allow such favouritism.

'Some for you,' he told Jane, 'and some for Mummy.'

Tony was quick to see someone poaching on his preserve.

'She's not your Mummy,' he told his cousin assertively. 'She's my Mummy.'

David considered this statement and then turned to Jane with a winning smile.

'Are you my Mummy?' he asked, as if the question had little significance, apart from a detached interest in a matter of fact.

'No, David. I'm afraid I'm not.' Jane's tone implied that the question was a perfectly normal one, but there was a lump in her throat as she answered.

'Have I got a Mummy?' enquired the young man with increasing interest.

'No, darling.' How could she explain the situation simply to the child? She glanced at Celia for help, but David supplied his own simple solution.

'Then you can be my Mummy.'

Jane noticed inconsequently that David's stammer had quite disappeared and only a slight hesitancy marred his babyish speech.

Tony, who had watched the exchange with interest, interrupted scornfully.

'No, she can't. Mummies have to belong to Daddies. She doesn't belong to your Daddy.'

David considered this piece of philosophy and then smiled confidently at Jane.

'I want her to belong to my Daddy,' he stated positively.

Celia laughed as she came to Jane's rescue.

'We shall have to see about that,' she told David non-committally. 'Now both get your things and we'll go indoors for tea.'

The promise of such an important event sent the two youngsters scampering to collect their scattered belongings; other thoughts receded, at least temporarily, before the anticipation of teatime delights.

'How beautifully simple life is at that age,' Celia remarked. When Jane did not answer, she continued as if speaking to herself. 'All the same, I'd glad that Duncan is thinking of marrying again. He needs to, as much for his own sake as for David's. I only hope that he has found the right woman this time.'

Jane felt her body stiffen as she listened to the words.

'Dr Frobisher is going to be married?' she asked haltingly.

'Oh, nothing as definite as that,' Celia responded. 'You know what a closed book Duncan can be. Last night, though, he said something which I think was a strong hint that he is thinking along those lines.' She laughed affectionately. 'That from Duncan is the most that we're likely to get until it is an accomplished fact.'

So this was the end of all her foolish imaginings, thought Jane. She did not for one moment doubt Celia's contention that a hint from Duncan was as good as an unqualified statement from most men.

Celia went on talking gaily as she speculated on the possibility of her brother's marriage.

'You know, Jane,' she said teasingly, 'I think David's idea is a brainwave. Duncan ought to marry you — it's so obviously right from everyone's point of view.' She glanced at Jane mischievously, but the girl beside her held a rigid pose expressionlessly.

Suddenly Celia laid a gentle hand on Jane's and her lovely face was full of sympathetic concern.

'Oh, my dear. I am so sorry. Believe me, I didn't realise.'

'It's all right,' said Jane. 'I mean, it doesn't matter.'

Each knew to what the other referred without explanation.

'But of course it matters,' insisted

Celia. 'What a fool I've been not to have noticed before.'

'Thank goodness you didn't. My pride has suffered enough already, and now you know!' Jane finished on a desperate note.

'You poor dear,' said Celia, with genuine sympathy. 'Believe me, Jane, nothing would make me happier than to see Duncan married to you. Oh, my dear, what a blundering ass I am! Please forgive me.'

Jane laughed uncertainly.

'Thank you for the compliment, Celia. It soothes my injured pride just a little.'

Celia's hand pressed gently on Jane's and expressed much that was not spoken. Impulsively Jane turned to Duncan's sister.

'Please, Celia, you won't mention this, even to Edward, will you? I couldn't bear it.'

Celia gave her hand a reassuring pat as she rose to meet the returning children.

'It's your secret, Jane, and I promise that I'll keep it for you.'

Jane smiled wanly. Celia still did not know that Duncan himself had already divined that secret, she reflected sadly as she led young David to his tea.

Nanny was still out and Celia was as happy as the children at the prospect of keeping her son company for nursery tea. The riot that ended the meal would have shocked the staid and competent Nanny, but it was thoroughly enjoyed by the four participants.

Jane was being a 'bucking bronco' for Tony when Edward Gresham and Duncan arrived at the nursery, guided by sounds of hilarious mirth. Tony ran to his father and cannoned against Edward's immaculately trousered legs, but David offered only a vague greeting. A confused and dishevelled Jane was restrained in a kneeling position by strenuous demands for his turn to ride. David's piping treble called to his father to watch the performance.

'She's going to be my Mummy,' he

announced, indicating the kneeling Jane.

There was a sudden silence in the room and Duncan's smile disappeared as his face returned to its familiar expressionless mould.

'What makes you think that?' he asked, in a voice which denied the sensational impact of his son's remark.

The young man considered for a moment and Celia would have interrupted but for an imperious gesture from her brother.

The cause of her consternation favoured Jane with his most cherubic smile. 'I want her to be,' he asserted.

Jane had been frozen into immobility by that first devastating remark. In her confusion she reacted instinctively by hugging the little boy and uttering a forced laugh.

'If wishes were horses beggars would ride,' she told the child, reverting to a well-worn nursery maxim in her embarrassment, before she sprang to her feet and made her escape through the door.

As she passed Celia, Jane threw the

other woman a pleading glance, but Tony's mother was not looking at her.

Jane remained in the room that had become her own until she was certain that she would find Celia alone, and then made her way to the other's room. On Nanny's day off it had become customary for Jane to spend the night with the Greshams, but she felt that she could not face Duncan again that day.

Celia was completely sympathetic with Jane's wish to avoid an embarrassing meeting, at least for that day, but she insisted that if Jane felt that she must go to her own home then Edward would drive her. No protest could deflect Celia from this point, so eventually Jane was forced, however reluctantly, to agree.

When, dressed for the street and carrying her overnight case, Jane descended to the hall, Celia was waiting for her.

'Off you go,' she urged in a conspiratorial whisper, 'the car is waiting, so hurry up. Your chauffeur mustn't be kept waiting.'

With a grateful smile, Jane ran down

the steps to where the Gresham's long, grey car was standing with the engine already running. The door was opened for her and she quickly seated herself beside the driver. The car was moving almost before she had closed the door, which made her feel that Edward Gresham probably considered this journey as an unnecessary interruption to an otherwise quiet evening.

'It is very good of you to take this trouble,' she said. 'I do appreciate it.'

As her companion spoke, Jane started violently.

'Not at all,' he said. 'Edward keeps his car so well that it is always a pleasure to borrow it on any excuse.' In the darkness beside her, Duncan chuckled. 'Another case of mistaken identity, Jane?' he enquired without taking his eyes from the road ahead.

'I did think that you were Mr Gresham when I got in,' she admitted.

'Just so,' responded her self-appointed driver enigmatically.

They continued to drive in silence

until Jane found a commonplace on which to base a remark.

'You've missed the turning,' she told him, 'but the next left will bring us out in the right place.'

'I doubt it,' remarked Duncan, as he drove past the turning with undiminished speed.

'But I often go that way,' protested Jane.

'Possibly, but not just now. When you are being kidnapped the most unusual things can happen.'

Her heart beat faster, but she did not protest again. She was completely in his power and it was no good fighting his will while he had control of the car.

As she sat beside him in unhappy silence, the comfortable hum of the engine gradually lulled her senses. It was surprising that Duncan, who could rouse and embarrass her so easily, could also, by his very presence, give her such a sense of stable security as she had never known before. By the time he drew the car into the courtyard of a wayside inn, a feeling of unreality was the strongest of her emotions.

With his usual uncommunicative manner he led her into a low-beamed dining room and ordered drinks for both of them without consulting her by word or action. Before there was a pause for conversation, a menu appeared. It was not until the first course of the meal was in front of them that they were alone once more. More dangerously alone than in the car, Jane thought. There at least she could say what she liked to him or take refuge in silence as she chose, but in the public dining room she was isolated with him and devoid of her chosen weapons.

She glanced across the table to find Duncan regarding her with quiet amusement. Hurriedly she put her hand out for the salt to avoid meeting his eyes. His hand met hers in the centre of the table and held it momentarily.

'Just forget the efficient Miss Marten for tonight, Jane. Let us just be a cosy couple taking a cosy meal at a cosy inn.'

Under the influence of that extraordinarily infectious smile her mood changed. She smiled back at him and chuckled almost happily.

'In cosy company?' she asked mischievously.

He laughed outright at that.

'I see you don't think the adjective suits me.'

'I can think of more apt descriptions,' she retorted with spirit.

'Hmm. Well, We won't pursue the matter,' he told her magnanimously.

'Thank you.'

For once he had allowed a chance to tease her slip by almost without notice.

Their meal proceeded in an atmosphere of uneasy but not unfriendly badinage until Jane found her earlier embarrassment in his company fading into the background of her thoughts.

When he had ordered coffee to be served in the comfortable lounge, Duncan led her purposefully to a deep sofa in a corner by the fireplace and seated himself beside her. Their coffee served and their cigarettes alight he sat forward and regarded her with quizzical scrutiny.

'Why do men and women try to work together?' he asked, of nobody in particular. 'Do you realise that this is only the second time that we have met as our true selves?'

Jane smiled uncertainly, unsure how to react to this mood of his.

'Do you really find me an impossible person, Jane?'

She considered the question carefully.

'Impossible is quite the wrong word,' she told him honestly. 'In fact I have enjoyed working for you most of the time.'

'Not for me,' he corrected. 'With me, but not for me.'

Jane laughed.

'I wish you could try working for yourself,' she told him. 'You would soon know that to work with Dr Frobisher is to work for him.'

'How should I translate that?' Does *for* in that sentence mean *under orders from* or does it mean *on the side of* — are you on my side, Jane?'

She was half amused and half distressed as she met his grey eyes.

'Usually I am,' she said, trying to be objective. 'But there are other times.'

'Times when you are on David's side, perhaps,' he suggested.

Jane realised that he was completely serious. She bit her lip, recognising the trap.

'I have always been on David's side,' she said quietly.

'And you still are today — about his solution to the mother problem?'

The room was very quiet and peaceful. There had only been one other party of coffee drinkers when they sat down and now those too had left. Only the sounds from the nearby bar broke the pregnant silence as Jane sought to frame her reply.

'He is only a baby. He didn't know what he was saying.' Her voice was small and tight, hardly recognisable.

'On the contrary, I think he knew exactly what he wanted and, very sensibly, he was taking the most direct course to his goal. I admit that he has stolen my thunder somewhat, but it doesn't really make too much difference.'

His words came in the clipped and precise manner that discussion of his private affairs always provoked. She looked at him in surprise and found her glance irresistibly held.

'Will you marry me, Jane?'

His tone was so natural and unsensational that she did not feel the impact of his words immediately. In that moment she hesitated, thinking confusedly of David. To him she was an accepted and trustworthy part of his life. He at least loved her with all his babyish confidence. If only she could be as sure of his father!

'Why?' she asked with serious emphasis.

His grey eyes widened with surprise as he met her challenging stare. He was obviously taken aback for the first time in their acquaintance.

'Well, because . . . ' He hesitated and Jane anticipated his reply.

'Because I would make a good mother for David?'

'Well, yes.'

For once the ground had been cut from under Duncan's feet and he was uncertain of himself.

'I see.' Her eyes blazed at him. 'You make me furious,' she declared. 'For all your arrogance and self-sufficiency you have not the slightest idea what you are doing with your life. David has ten times your sense. He knows what he wants and he asks for it in a straight-forward manner. But you — yes, you *are* impossible. If you want me to be a full-time mother substitute for David then please say so. But don't ask me to make a lovable little boy a reason for marrying his father.'

'There are other reasons for marrying,' he told her with amused emphasis.

Jane hesitated for a moment, but she was too much roused to resist the challenge in his eyes.

'Yes,' she agreed. 'There are other reasons, as you so rightly say. Good, honest, wonderful reasons. There are also stupid, self-indulgent reasons that bear no relation to love and the beauty of what marriage should be.'

Duncan leaned back on the seat beside her and closed his eyes.

'Are you trying to tell me that, in your eyes, I stand condemned for having married for the wrong reasons once?'

She gasped involuntarily.

'Oh, no!' she exclaimed earnestly. 'I'm sorry, I didn't mean . . . ' His hand covered hers gently.

'Of course you didn't, Jane. I spoke without thinking.'

She laughed shakily.

'How often do you do that?' she asked.

'Not often,' he admitted. 'You should take it as a compliment that I let an uncensored thought pass in your company.'

'I take it as the greatest compliment that you could ever pay me,' she told him sincerely.

He smiled at her and she knew that if nothing else came from this evening they had at least established an under-standing far deeper than they had ever known before.

She looked down at their clasped hands and realised for the first time that her fingers had closed on his as she had tried desperately to communicate her convictions to him. His eyes followed the direction of her glance and a sardonic smile crossed his face.

'Any casual observer could be excused for believing us to be an engaged couple,' he observed.

Jane passed her tongue over suddenly dry lips.

'You must know that I couldn't make David a reason for marrying,' she said quietly.

'Quite so.' His tone was expression-less. 'But there is another side to it — my side. I may not be a very exciting suitor for your romantic heart, but I can offer you a reasonably comfortable life and — considerable affection, my dear.'

She smiled wistfully. As he sat beside her, she felt the security of his presence as an almost tangible thing. In his present all but humble mood he was very dear, but now that the time for decision had come, she was surprised at her own calm ability to resist the temptation to take what he was offering and be happy with the second best.

'A comfortable life and considerable affection,' she echoed regretfully.

'You don't find it enough?'

She shook her head sadly. 'There should be more to marriage than that,' she told him.

'We could find the rest together.' His tone was so gently persuasive that for a moment she hesitated, but only for a moment.

'No,' she said with quiet firmness. 'That is the wrong way. Find it first, and then you will be sure that you have found the right person to share the other things.'

He rose abruptly.

'We may as well go,' he said tersely.

The homeward drive was silent and uneventful. It was not until the car stood motionless by her own home that Duncan spoke again.

'Do you want to go in or will you come back with me? You can forget tonight completely if you want to. I will try my best not to remind you.' He smiled at her wryly.

'I think I would rather stay here tonight.'

This was the hardest parting ever. Her heart cried out to her not to let him go — how could she be so foolish as to relinquish all that she had dreamed of? To be near to him and with him would surely be enough. But she knew that without his love to complete her own all the rest would be empty and meaningless in the long years that must follow the first delight.

Unconsciously she was gazing at him as these thoughts tumbled through her mind, until he turned to smile at her again.

'Have you ever been in love, Jane?'

She faltered, but now she had a new-found courage with which to face him.

'Yes,' she replied simply.

'So you know what you mean when you tell me to find love before I marry? I suppose that is what you were telling me.'

'Yes. That is what I was trying to say, and I do know what I mean.'

He lifted her hand to his lips and kissed it.

'Would it be stealing if I kissed you properly?' His voice was gently teasing.

'It would,' she said aloud, but inwardly her heart cried out — 'You can only steal what is not yours already.' She had spoken as emphatically as she was able but she could not meet his eyes.

'You always flinch when you try to lie, Jane. Remember that. You are too honest to be happy even with little white lies.'

She looked down at her hands unhappily as he walked round the car and led her to the door of her home.

'I am going away for a few days tomorrow,' he told her. 'Look after David until I get back. Goodnight, my dear.'

Once again she had lost her chance to make a decisive gesture of parting. The powerful car gathered speed into the darkness.

* * *

In the days that followed Duncan's departure, Jane sometimes wondered whether she had imagined his startling proposal. From Celia she learned that he was in London on business concerned with his new appointment. When he would return nobody seemed to know.

Celia was, if possible, more friendly than before. The thought of parting from this new friend so soon added to Jane's regrets as she prepared her retreat. She studied all the columns of vacancies for posts to which her qualifications would suit her. All that she required of a job was that the work should be hard enough to absorb all her attention, and that it should put as much distance as possible between herself and everything associated with Duncan Frobisher.

Try as she would to avoid it, she found herself inevitably drawn into the life of the Gresham family and their acceptance of her was too warm to be cast aside with seeming ingratitude. It was with Duncan that she must make the break, and the opportunity to do so was continually denied to her as Celia persistently avoided giving her his address in London. Too self-conscious to insist, Jane could only wait impatiently until the knowledge came her way.

With Tony back at his school in the daytime and Nanny in constant attendance, Jane's care of David was no more than nominal. She found that most of her time was spent in helping Celia with the work of the many committees and associations to which she belonged. Whenever Jane raised the subject of her strange position, Celia countered that Duncan would never forgive her if David were parted from his beloved Jane. It was indeed a strange position, Jane reflected, that she should find herself in very much the same relationship to Duncan's child as Celia had with her own little son. Duncan Frobisher certainly knew how to get his own way. She had refused to marry him solely to take the place of David's dead mother, so he had skilfully manoeuvred her into that position by denying her the chance to do anything else. She knew too that she was already dangerously fond of the little boy.

When Celia announced that she intended to drive down to Ives to see that all her instructions of the previous visit had been carried out, Jane was only too glad for another chance to spend a few hours at Duncan's beautiful home. They set out early in the morning and it was scarcely noon when Celia turned the car into the drive that led to the old house.

Jane slipped from the car and stood gazing at the mellow front of the long, low house. This, she told herself, was the real goodbye. To the house she could be as sentimental as she pleased. It would never tell if she even shed a secret tear in its empty rooms while Celia was busy elsewhere. In her handbag was a letter which had arrived that morning offering her a teaching post in Canada. She had no doubt about the wording of the cable that would take her reply. Canada was the land of opportunity for youth, she had often been told, and she was still young. Young enough to find a cure for a so-called broken heart.

With forced cheerfulness, she followed Celia into the house only to come to an amazed halt in the low-beamed entrance hall.

Standing facing them was Duncan Frobisher.

Celia was the first to recover from her obviously genuine surprise.

'I thought you were in London,' she told her brother with mixed pleasure and annoyance.

'So I was,' he replied blandly, 'and I

would have been there still if you hadn't been so kind as to tell Edward about this proposed visit.'

'Well, what are you doing here, anyway?' demanded his sister.

Duncan smiled at her boyishly.

'Waiting to greet you of course,' he told her. 'There is a reasonable cold lunch on the table, so let's start with that.'

Jane had not uttered a word nor had he spoken to her directly, but it was her arm that he took to lead the way to the dining room.

During the meal Jane told them both of her letter from Canada.

'Very interesting,' was Duncan's sole comment, with which he dismissed the subject, quelling any protest from Celia with a stern glance. He asked questions about their joint activities during the past days as if the subject really intrigued him and firmly refused to allow either of the women to gain the initiative in the conversation.

When the meal was over, Duncan

rose and escorted them from the room, every inch the perfect host. In the entrance hall he turned to his sister.

'It was very good of you to come all this way on my behalf, Celia. I am very grateful. You should get home before dark quite easily if you start now.'

Celia opened her mouth to speak and closed it suddenly. A slight smile flickered in her eyes.

'You will bring Jane back I suppose?' she asked conversationally.

'Naturally,' he replied.

It was Jane's turn to protest, but his detaining hand on her arm commanded her silence until Celia had waved a gloved hand as her car turned out of the drive. When the car was finally out of sight, Duncan turned to Jane with a smile that suddenly reminded her of David.

'And now at last we can talk in decent privacy and comfort.'

'But there is really nothing to talk about,' she said. 'I have told you that I shall be leaving for Canada in two week's time. That's all there is to say.'

'Really?' He was obviously not impressed by her assertion. 'Well, now, I will tell you what you will be doing in two week's time. Come in here.' He led the way into the large drawing room.

As she entered the room, her eyes involuntarily sought the place where the disturbing portrait of his dead wife had hung when she last visited Ives. Though she corrected her mistake almost instantly, Duncan's eyes had followed her glance.

'A doubtful piece of tact on Celia's part,' he remarked.

'Would it have worried you?' she enquired shyly.

'No.' The reply was terse. 'But it might have disturbed my future wife.'

The words had a definite emphasis and Jane stiffened involuntarily.

'Come here, Jane,' he commanded unnecessarily, as she was standing by his side. His arms closed about her strongly. 'In two week's time you will not be setting off for Canada or any other such place. You will be Mrs Duncan Frobisher and you will be wherever your husband is at that time.' His lips closed on hers. It was the kiss of a man both gentle and hard, giving and demanding.

Breathlessly Jane faced him, still held firmly in his encircling arms.

'You can't do this,' she gasped. 'Not to me or to any woman.'

He laughed gently. 'Can't I?' he asked. She met his eyes that were both mocking and tender and she knew that he could. She would marry him in spite of her resolutions. His will was too strong for her to resist against her own inclinations.

'You will marry me, Jane?' The inflection was questioning but the words constituted a statement rather than a question.

She nodded dumbly.

He lifted her face gently as his arm held her even closer.

'Dear, sweet Jane,' he said softly. 'Will you forgive me one day?'

'I don't know. Even now I don't know.'

He kissed her again softly and tenderly, but there was no warmth in her response, only quiet resignation. He drew away from her and turned abruptly.

'You had better go and tidy yourself, as women put it,' he said expressionlessly. 'Even on this auspicious occasion, I have things to do. We shall meet for tea.'

He was gone before she could reply.

Too stunned for tears, Jane stood gazing through the windows to where a steady drizzle blurred the scene. The meadow, the trees and the river were all there just as before, but the sunlight was gone. Inwardly she cried, 'My dear love. How can I ever find you?' Had she really committed herself to him without a word of love passing between them? She gazed unseeingly into the room until it gradually came into focus. Such a beautiful room — a fool's paradise, she told herself bitterly.

The afternoon slipped by unheeded

until the fading light drew her attention to the passing time. Where was he now, she wondered. How would he greet her when he returned? Roused out of her reflective mood, she decided to explore the house. If she was to make it her home, it would be as well to know her way about, she told herself with wry humour. The housekeeper had returned to her cottage after their lunch so she would have the house to herself until Duncan returned.

She wandered through the empty rooms. The whole place had an air of patient waiting. Every room was in orderly, shining readiness; ready to come to life when it was asked to make a home once more. There was something very sad about this air of patient waiting.

Jane's steps led her eventually into a small library. In this room as in no other, Duncan's influence was obvious. Smilingly she reflected that one library was much like another and, after all, it was in just such a room that she had met the man she loved so much. Yet she was conscious of his influence in this room so strongly that she caught her breath involuntarily. Even his dog was waiting, she thought, with a catch in her throat as she caught sight of the broad back of an elderly terrier who lay in front of the cheerful fire, half hidden by the great armchair that faced the fireplace. His piano, too — how little she knew of this beloved man. The presence of a piano in his library argued that it was probable that he spent some leisure moments at the keyboard, and yet he had never mentioned a love of music to her or admitted an ability to play any instrument.

Slowly she raised the piano lid and musingly stroked the keys. Some gave gently under her touch and their notes echoed softly round the darkening room. Tempted by the sound, she allowed her hands to find a series of chords and stray into a melody; a Bach prelude, a Chopin nocturne, the lovely Andante theme from Tchaikovsky's Fifth Symphony — arranged for piano by some unknown devotee. How long she played she did not know. Jane had never considered herself a more than adequate pianist, but on that afternoon her whole soul flowed into the music that her hands evoked. When at last she paused, the room was dark except for the fire-light. She looked down to find that the dog had left his place by the fire to sit at her feet. The old terrier looked up at her enquiringly while silence flowed back into the room.

'Yes, boy,' she said gently. 'You understand, don't you? Go and find your master, boy. Go and tell him.' The dog pricked his ear and regarded her with eyes bright with canine intelligence. Jane laughed almost happily. 'You would if you could, wouldn't you?' she asked him conversationally. 'You would tell him that we're all waiting — you, old friend, his home, his son — and me, too.' Her voice was no more than a whisper as she spoke the last words. She dropped to her knees and fondled the dog's hairy head. 'Go and tell him,' she pleaded.

'Tell him we're waiting, and give him all my love; every little bit, boy, remember that.'

They sat on the floor together, the dog and the girl, and looked at each other over the gulf of intellect that separates man and beast.

'Well, Mike. Do as the lady says.' Duncan's voice came through the darkness.

Jane stood up slowly. A feeling of inevitability pervaded the atmosphere of the quiet room. Apprehensively she glanced around, but the dim light showed no familiar shadow standing watching her. With an unsteady hand she switched on the lamp on the piano. A pool of brilliance sprang to life about her, but showed no more than the empty room. Wonderingly she looked back at the dog who looked from her to the fire and back again before he turned and padded back to his original place on the hearth rug.

With dawning understanding, Jane watched the terrier as he stood looking up at the chair that was turned to the fire. Suddenly she knew that Duncan was sitting there, hidden by the great back of the chair.

As she stood, speechless and trembling, his long form unfolded and came towards her.

'Jane.' His voice was pitched very low.

She tried to speak, but her mouth was dry. No words came.

Gently he led her to the fire and placed her in the great chair which had hidden him from her view. He seated himself on the broad arm, looking down at her.

'What — where have you been?' she asked weakly. The question had little meaning but it broke the silence between them.

He chose to consider her words seriously.

'Where have I been?' he repeated. 'Well, now, I wonder where I was? I think I must have been escaping somewhere.'

'Escaping?' she queried.

'Escaping from myself, but thinking

too. Thinking of my future wife. A very lovely wife, with big brown eyes that have the power to look right into my very soul if only they would see it.'

The silence of the house was no longer cold. An intimate warmth crept round them while time stood still.

'And what were you thinking about her, Duncan?' Jane's heart beat wildly as she waited for his reply.

'I was thinking that she is good and kind, gentle and humorous, but that I hardly know her at all. Yes, I was thinking all that and that she would be a wonderful mother for my son.'

A spark of hope that had sprung to life in Jane's heart fluttered and died. She hardly heard the softly spoken words as his voice continued on the edge of her consciousness.

'I was also thinking that it is little wonder that everyone loves you, Jane. First it was Celia, then Max. I was amused at their enthusiasm — I must admit that. And then you came to the Villa Alto. You took Mary from me; she had always been my nearest friend and only confidante until you arrived. Mario — I had always been a bit of a hero to Mario until you stole his heart too. You come to my home and it springs into a new life in your presence. Then to crown your list of sins you seduce my dog with your music.' There was a long pause.

'And you, Duncan?' she asked. 'What have I done to you?'

'You have taken my whole life into those small hands of yours, Jane.'

Jane stood up slowly. She drew a long breath and discovered that she was trembling again. Why did her legs always threaten to give way when she most needed their support? In spite of the cheerful fire, she was cold again; cold and hurt and infinitely sad.

'And now,' she said in a small voice, 'I am to be trusted with your life and David's. I am to marry you to be your . . . ' she paused uncertainly, 'your companion and your son's mother. That is what you ask in return for what you have to give to me. Is that it, Duncan?'

'If that is all that you have to offer, Jane.' He took her hands between his. 'Is that all, my dear?'

'I don't understand you.' Her words tumbled out, quickly and breathlessly.

'I am inclined to think you do.' His smile was tender. Every touch of his hands was a caress that increased the trembling of her slight body.

'Duncan, please . . . I want to understand. Really I do.'

'Let me tell you then that I too can wait. Just as you and all your conquests that you were telling Mike about can wait. I can wait for my wife.'

'Please — please let me go.' She pulled her hands from his, but a painfully strong grip held her firmly.

Appealingly she looked up into the darkly handsome face above her own. Tears of pleading welled in her eyes as she met his steady gaze.

'No, Jane. That I will never do. I will never let you go now.' He drew her irresistibly into his arms until her head rested against his shoulder. His voice was low and indistinct, as she had never heard it before.

'Jane, my darling,' he murmured. 'I love you so much.'

She felt his heart beating against her own. She had found her longed-for happiness and it had an undreamed of sweetness. Suddenly she knew something else. He had spoken those words before and his love had been cruelly mistreated; little wonder that he had found it so hard to speak the same words again.

At last she understood why it had taken so long for those simple words to find a voice. To admit to loving again, to invite for a second time the torment that had filled his life once before, required a degree of courage which made even the dauntless Duncan Frobisher question his own wisdom.

She drew away from him until she could see his face.

'Thank you, my darling,' she murmured. 'Thank you with all my heart.'

He laughed a little unsteadily as he

held her closely.

'For what am I being thanked so fervently?' he asked with amused tenderness.

'For the gift of your trust, my dearest.' Instinctively she put a hand against his tanned cheek. 'I shall always cherish it.'

A tentative 'woof' drew their attention to the dog at their feet. He sat back on his broad haunches regarding them brightly, his head on one side. Plainly he was enquiring what part he had in this affair. Jane and Duncan laughed delightedly at him.

'Yes, old man. You are the hero of this piece,' Duncan told him. 'If she hadn't won your heart too we would now be acting a formal 'tea for two' scene with an uncomfortably polite sequel. But now — now it's going to be very different.' He turned to Jane, a mischievous smile lifting the corners of his mouth.

Her heart beat a joyful tattoo. 'He can certainly be devilish if he likes' she thought with delighted surprise at this discovery of yet another facet of his character.